S0-BSF-544

Jake reached out, stroked the side of her face.

"I always pictured you in perpetual sunshine," he whispered, his voice a caress.

Tess swallowed hard, trying to ignore his fingertips as they grazed a sensitive spot beneath her jaw. "No one lives that way, Jake, but I've finally found the life I was meant for."

"I'm glad," he said, slipping his hand away. He turned, moved to make his way back to work. Tess stared at the proud, determined line of his spine as he drew himself to his full height, and knew she had been pushed to her limit.

"Don't." She reached out and touched his arm, her fingertips meeting warm male skin. He turned, slipped his arm around her.

"Don't what?" he whispered, but Tess was beyond thought. All she could register was Jake's steely strength around her.

"Don't," she simply repeated, but the word sounded like a promise, an invitation.

Dear Reader,

What a special lineup of love stories Silhouette Romance has for you this month. Bestselling author Sandra Steffen continues her BACHELOR GULCH miniseries with *Clayton's Made-Over Mrs.* And in *The Lawman's Legacy*, favorite author Phyllis Halldorson introduces a special promotion called MEN! Who says good men are hard to find?! Plus, we've got Julianna Morris's *Daddy Woke up Married*—our BUNDLES OF JOY selection—*Love, Marriage and Family 101* by Anne Peters, *The Scandalous Return of Jake Walker* by Myrna Mackenzie and *The Cowboy Who Broke the Mold* by Cathleen Galitz, who makes her Silhouette debut as one of our WOMEN TO WATCH.

I hope you enjoy all six of these wonderful novels. In fact, I'd love to get your thoughts on Silhouette Romance. If you'd like to share your comments about the Silhouette Romance line, please send a letter directly to my attention: Melissa Senate, Senior Editor, Silhouette Books, 300 E. 42nd St., 6th Floor, New York, NY 10017. I welcome all of your comments, and here are a few particulars I'd like to have your feedback on:
1) Why do you enjoy Silhouette Romance?
2) What types of stories would you like to see more of? Less of?
3) Do you have favorite authors?

Your thoughts about Romance are very important to me. After all, these books are for you! Again, I hope you enjoy our six novels this month—and that you'll write me with your thoughts.

Regards,

Melissa Senate
Senior Editor
Silhouette Books

Please address questions and book requests to:
Silhouette Reader Service
U.S.: 3010 Walden Ave., P.O. Box 1325, Buffalo, NY 14269
Canadian: P.O. Box 609, Fort Erie, Ont. L2A 5X3

THE SCANDALOUS
RETURN OF JAKE WALKER

Myrna Mackenzie

Silhouette
R O M A N C E™
Published by Silhouette Books
America's Publisher of Contemporary Romance

If you purchased this book without a cover you should be aware that this book is stolen property. It was reported as "unsold and destroyed" to the publisher, and neither the author nor the publisher has received any payment for this "stripped book."

To Jimmie and Suzette, thank you for all the laughter, lunches and all the times you just listened when I needed you to. Special friends like you are rare. (Just wanted you to know that I noticed.)

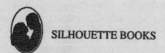 SILHOUETTE BOOKS

ISBN 0-373-19256-8

THE SCANDALOUS RETURN OF JAKE WALKER

Copyright © 1997 by Myrna Topol

All rights reserved. Except for use in any review, the reproduction or utilization of this work in whole or in part in any form by any electronic, mechanical or other means, now known or hereafter invented, including xerography, photocopying and recording, or in any information storage or retrieval system, is forbidden without the written permission of the editorial office, Silhouette Books, 300 East 42nd Street, New York, NY 10017 U.S.A.

All characters in this book have no existence outside the imagination of the author and have no relation whatsoever to anyone bearing the same name or names. They are not even distantly inspired by any individual known or unknown to the author, and all incidents are pure invention.

This edition published by arrangement with Harlequin Books S.A.

® and TM are trademarks of Harlequin Books S.A., used under license. Trademarks indicated with ® are registered in the United States Patent and Trademark Office, the Canadian Trade Marks Office and in other countries.

Printed in U.S.A.

Books by Myrna Mackenzie

Silhouette Romance

The Baby Wish #1046
The Daddy List #1090
Babies and a Blue-Eyed Man #1182
The Secret Groom #1225
The Scandalous Return of Jake Walker #1256

MYRNA MACKENZIE

Winner of the Holt Medallion Award honoring outstanding literary talent, Myrna Mackenzie has always been fascinated by the belief that within every man is a hero, and inside every woman lives a heroine. She loves to write about ordinary people making extraordinary dreams come true. A former teacher, Myrna lives in the suburbs of Chicago with her husband—who was her high school sweetheart—and her two sons. She believes in love, laughter, music, vacations to the mountains, watching the stars, anything unattached to the words *physical fitness* and letting dust balls gather where they may. Readers can write to Myrna at P.O. Box 225, LaGrange, IL 60525-0225.

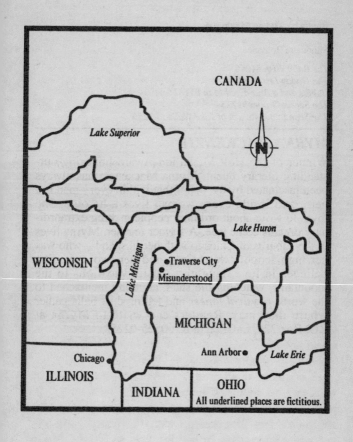

CANADA

Lake Superior

Lake Huron

WISCONSIN

Lake Michigan

•Traverse City

Misunderstood

MICHIGAN

Chicago •

Ann Arbor •   *Lake Erie*

ILLINOIS

INDIANA

OHIO

All underlined places are fictitious.

Chapter One

Jake Walker still looked like liquid sin poured into pants, Tess Buchanan thought, closing her front door and moving toward the shirtless man dominating the crumbling porch of the house across the road. Eleven years hadn't changed that, but it *was* a long time. He would have met a lot of people, done a lot of living during those years. What were the chances he would remember who she was?

Slim. Very slim.

"Let's hope that's true," Tess murmured, curling her nails into her palms. If he remembered her face—or her name—her task would be that much more difficult. And she didn't feel like dealing with "difficult" just now, not when everything in her life was so...right. She finally had security, respect, a near-perfect future, she thought, remembering the wedding dresses she'd looked at last week. "Difficult" just didn't fit into the picture.

Studying the man who had bent on one knee to examine the damage to the rotting boards of his porch, he didn't look like a potential problem—until one noted the hard line of his jaw, the underlying power in his body. And when he stood again as he was doing now, there was a lethal grace to his movements. He was long, lean, but strong. Not a man you'd want to annoy.

She'd definitely annoyed him. Heck, she'd done a lot more than that. And even if he didn't remember her, he'd remember that she'd messed up his life, however unwillingly.

Tess registered that thought. She forced herself to continue walking toward Jake. When she'd first seen him she'd been a naive, too-intelligent kid who'd bypassed years of school and had come to the town of Misunderstood, Michigan to observe real teachers in action, a prelude to her teacher training. She'd been a teenager among teenagers, but...different. A child playing dress-up, too soap-dish clean in her pretend teacher garb amid the other kids dressed blue-jean casual.

An invisible student, she'd watched the teachers, but also Jake. From a distance. Shyly. She'd dismissed his dangerous reputation, dreamed a young girl's dreams, held her breath when he neared her in the sea of students traversing the hall.

But they'd never really met.

And she'd been wrong to dismiss that reputation. She'd seen that the day her path had finally collided with his.

Remembering, Tess forced air in and out of her lungs. She purposefully pushed open the gate that led from her yard as she took the steps that would take her into Jake's path again. She smoothed trembling fingers down her biscuit-colored skirt, holding them there until the shaking stopped.

"Keep going, Buchanan," she ordered herself. "He's

just a man. This is only business. Nothing more." And what the heck, time changed everything. She'd returned to the town she'd learned to love, made a home and a significant place for herself here. She was wiser. They were both much older.

But some things remained the same. Jake Walker still had that long, shaggy midnight hair.

The thought startled her. If *she* remembered that....

She moved closer. He loomed larger.

He was obviously still reckless and tempting fate, she thought, noting the Harley in the weed-choked yard. The motorcycle's rumble had awakened her at midnight and she hadn't slept since. The knowledge that this moment, this meeting, really was inevitable had kept her far too edgy to relax.

Skirting the swirling puddles where rain had fallen earlier, Tess made it to the middle of the pockmarked road. Halfway between her house and his, she looked up, straight into the cool green eyes of the man who had obviously noticed her. He leaned back against the house, his bare skin against the rough clapboards as he watched her careful approach.

They'd stood this way before, staring, taking each other's measure.

For half a heartbeat that thought and Jake's lazy inspection made Tess falter, then she pushed herself to take the next step. He was taller than she remembered, his shoulders broader and more heavily muscled. She remembered those shoulders because his shirt had been down around his elbows when she'd come upon him in that storage closet at school that day. She'd been sent for supplies, but what she'd found had been Jake with his hand up a girl's dress. An eighteen-year-old Jake making love, locked in Cassie Pratt's embrace, and looking at Tess with lightning and ice in those worldly-wise green eyes of his.

Tess stared back at Jake and raised her chin. She'd done nothing wrong. Not today, not then. *She* hadn't been the one making love in a public school.

The thought nearly made her stumble. It reminded her of the way she'd felt standing there staring at Jake. Stupid to have felt betrayed when she hadn't even known him, when she'd been warned about him, when he'd clearly been so intent on having Cassie that he'd broken into a locked closet.

"Old news, Tess," she whispered to herself, pushing onward. No need to be nervous now. She wasn't that foolish kid anymore. Jake had never known about her girlhood fantasies, and besides, *she* hadn't been the one in the wrong that day.

But she *had* been the one who had stood there, helpless to move as she held that door open, exposing the vulnerable couple inside instead of closing it as she should have. She'd been the one who'd felt guilt along with her disillusionment. Like a voyeur, a snitch in the end even if it *had* been Cassie who had shrieked and brought everyone running. Still...

Cassie had been pregnant. Jake had abandoned her. The thought flitted into Tess's mind and she pushed it aside. For the moment. Thinking about that would only make her angry, and she couldn't indulge her anger. Not now. They had business to tend to. He would need to be cooperative, so would she.

Her careful handling of the situation was key, even without the hurdle of Jake recognizing her. Because she knew for a fact that he didn't want to be here. She'd been told that he'd been trouble since the day he'd pushed his way into the world, but there would be no trouble today. This meeting would be different from their last. She was in control, and she would *not* be getting Jake expelled from school today.

She'd already done that.

That was the last she'd seen of him. The stolen keys found inside the closet had been damning evidence and justice had been swift. Tess had always felt she should have said something more—or less—than she had during the interrogation. She should have tried to help. But she'd done nothing. And Jake had made no attempt to speak at all, except when Cassie's sentence had been handed out. He'd silently shook his head at Cassie when they'd thrown him out. Hours later that same day he'd left town, and he hadn't been back since.

But now he was here, moving to the rickety rail, leaning down over her as she stepped close to his house.

He raised one lazy brow, lifted one corner of his lips slightly. He waited.

And in that second, Tess knew she'd been wrong. There was trouble, challenge, written all over Jake Walker, from those lean hips that made him look like a living ad for physical relationships to that gleam in his eye, that I-don't-give-a-damn half smile.

She'd known too many men who didn't give a damn. Her father. Her former husband. She'd survived them, and her years of teaching had even taught her that challenges could be fun. A troublesome kid could become a willing student, even a friend, if she handled the situation with care and caring.

Tess took a deep breath, looked up, way up. Her gaze snagged on Jake's again. This man was no troublesome child. He was pure male, muscle and bone and testosterone—and an eyeful of I-dare-you-to-cross-this-line.

She wasn't into dares, not at all, but she had a job to do. She darn well intended to do it.

Tess touched her toe to the scarred wood of the porch stairs.

"Don't even bother." His voice was a low growl.

She stopped dead before she'd managed to place her foot fully on the first step.

"Lady, I don't know who you are or what you're doing, but I've got to tell you, if you're the law, I'm clean. If you're selling something, I don't want any, and if you're looking for a good time, I'm not in the market right this moment. Try coming back later."

For two seconds Tess's heart stopped. She could swear that it did. For half a breath she considered running, turning tail and marching straight back across the street and into her house.

But that just wasn't her way. She had come to do a job and do a job she would, whether Jake Walker liked it or not.

With only guts and determination guiding her, she stepped up fully onto the stair and worked her way up the next two steps to the porch. She placed her hand on the railing next to Jake's hand.

"Mister, my name is not 'lady' and it never will be," she said slowly, succinctly, in a voice that had cowed many a six-foot-tall, hulking eighteen-year-old male. "It's Tess Buchanan, and I'm not the law, a salesperson, or a woman in search of a 'good time.'"

Jake looked down at the little bit of a woman standing before him. She was bristling like an indignant kitten. Her sleek brown hair was shot with red and gold and grazed her shoulders, swinging forward in a neat curtain when she moved as she was now. A tailored jacket nipped in her waist; a delicate gold butterfly on a chain emphasized the pale skin revealed by the wide lapels; a pencil-slender skirt kissed her knees. She had nice legs. Very nice legs.

"Not ever?" He lifted his lips in a shadow of a grin as he rubbed one hand across his jaw.

She blinked hard, tipping her head back as she looked up at him. "Not ever what?"

"You're not looking for a good time—ever?"

Jake watched her hands curl closed then open as she kept her chin high. Sweet pink crept up from beneath the ivory collar of her blouse. He wondered who in hell she was and what she was doing here. He hadn't expected to run into anyone but building inspectors and hardware store junkies during his short stay here. So maybe she was a real-estate agent anticipating a future sale—or maybe just some do-gooder schoolteacher type out to warn him to behave himself while he was in town.

Could be. That suit, the arms she'd just crossed, her slender feet that were planted just far enough apart to look purposeful, all spoke of a woman on a mission. Only the errant wisp of hair that had fallen awry, caressing her cheek, looked out of place. It made her seem young, slightly vulnerable, like she could use a little assistance from him.

Too bad he wasn't into community service. Still, for some reason he couldn't explain, he reached for the white shirt he'd left on the rickety swing and eased it over his shoulders.

He didn't miss her look of relief or the way his action seemed to free those pink lips that had stalled at his insulting comment earlier. She opened her mouth to begin her speech.

No way. He'd been dragged to this town against his will, but now that he was here he intended to make one thing clear. He didn't want every "good citizen" in town showing up on his doorstep.

"So," he began, crossing his arms over his still-unbuttoned shirt. "You want to tell me just who exactly Tess Buchanan is and why you're here at my house at—" he looked at his watch "—eight in the morning?"

It was as if someone had taken a pin and popped an already fading balloon. All the fight just slipped right out of her with a sigh. She shook her head slightly, blew out a breath. She held out her hand.

"I'm—sorry," she said suddenly. "Forgive my bad manners and my unfortunate timing. I'm—I'm the Chairwoman of the Historic Preservation Committee, and I'm here because I've been informed that you've decided to restore this house. Maybe you'd like me to come back later."

He raised his lips in that same lazy grin that had made her angry before.

"To talk about the house," she amended, clearly remembering his suggestion that she return later for that promised "good time." She kept her chin high even though she was obviously nervous. He had to give her credit.

Jake rested one hip against the rail. He tilted his head. "So you've heard I've decided to restore the house. What else have you heard? I'm curious. It's funny how a story changes in the retelling, isn't it?"

That got her. She pulled her hand back, clamped it against her side. "You're not here about the house?" she asked, and Jake noted the disbelief in her words. He also noticed the low, sensual thrum of her voice. It had nagged at him from the second she'd first opened her mouth. It seemed...familiar somehow, but then, that wasn't a possibility. Misunderstood was a small town. If he'd known her, he would have remembered. No, she was new, new being relative to the eleven years since he'd been here, anyway.

"Mr. Walker?" she asked again.

Jake arched one brow at the challenge in her voice. He held his hands out in surrender.

"Okay, you're right about that part. I *am* Jake Walker," he admitted, reluctantly taking the hand she had offered again, curving his fingers around her own. Her skin was virgin soft, an intriguing contrast to her husky voice and her strictly business appearance. Nerves he'd almost forgotten he had tingled, jumped. The urge to pull back quickly was sudden and strong, but Jake had learned to curb his urges. Slowly he unfurled his fingers and slid his palm away from hers as skin dragged against skin.

It was damn tempting to wipe that tingling away by rubbing his palm against his jeans, but he resisted and slipped his thumbs into his belt loops instead.

"What I meant, Ms. Buchanan, was that if you've been told that *I've* decided to restore this house, then you haven't done your homework." He raised one corner of his lips in a silent dare. "That decision wasn't made by me. I was told that if I didn't repair the premises, the house would be condemned. That rates as an ultimatum in my book."

Tess Buchanan crossed her arms. "And in mine, Mr. Walker. But as you can see, this house has gotten to be an eyesore. You left the town no choice."

She was right. Staring at the wobbly porch supports he could see that he should have taken care of things long before now. That didn't mean he liked the situation. He didn't like being back in Misunderstood at all.

Jake tilted his head in assent. "I intend to do what's

necessary, Ms. Buchanan, if that's what you're here to find out.''

Her lips curved upward just a touch. She seemed to relax—a bit. Her wariness dropped—slightly. Tess Buchanan opened her eyes wide and looked up at him as if he'd just granted her a pardon when she'd been expecting a life sentence.

Her eyes were violet—rare, vivid violet. Eyes that a man wouldn't forget once he'd seen them up close. Jake knew in a heartbeat that he *had* seen them before—and he knew where. In a different world, a different time, she'd stared back at him, startled, shaking, embarrassed by what could have only been deemed a damning situation. He'd watched those same soft eyes flicker as Tess Buchanan had answered the questions that had been asked of her in the only way someone like her ever could. Truthfully.

The next day he'd been miles away. He'd never seen those eyes again. But still he remembered them.

He wondered if *she* remembered *him*.

''That's great, then,'' she said, holding on to her soft smile. ''There's so much that needs to be done to bring this place back to its former glory.''

The words didn't sound much like what he'd envisioned when he'd decided that he couldn't let his mother's home be torn down. And he couldn't do that. Flora Walker hadn't had much pleasure in life. He and his father had seen to that. He alone had stolen her last dream of seeing him graduate, and then tried to remove the gossip from her life by removing *himself* from Misunderstood. In its own way, his departure from town had worked. He'd kept in touch, sent for his mother now and then, and anyway, it had been all he'd been able to do at the time. But now he could do one thing more. He

could repair the home she'd loved and that he'd allowed
to fall into abandon. If he fixed the place up, someone
would cherish it the way his mother had. But the words
"former glory" didn't figure into the equation.

"I know this wasn't your choice, but I assure you that
this is going to be a rewarding project," she told him.
"I wouldn't say so if it weren't true."

Jake looked down at the lady standing in front of him.
She looked absolutely innocent, trying to reassure him
that way. And she was a lot prettier smiling at him like
that than she'd been looking doe-eyed scared eleven
springs ago. Yet he had the definite feeling that there
was a failure to communicate going on here. He still
wasn't sure why the lady was standing on his doorstep
at eight in the morning looking like she was on her way
to church.

He smiled wryly, looked around him at the peeling
paint, the loose clapboards of the house.

This was no church—and he was not known as a vir-
tuous man. Not by a long shot. Why the hell had some-
body let this exuberant innocent loose within five miles
of him? With eyes and a face like hers, with a smile that
could make a man's knees useless for the task of holding
up his legs, the lady needed a keeper. Definitely.

"Ms. Buchanan?" Jake said, clearing his voice and
his thoughts. He took that moment to notice that she was
wearing a small diamond on her left hand. So she did
have a keeper of sorts, someone who had plans for the
lady's future—didn't she? Where in heaven's name was
the man? Didn't he know who Jake Walker was? Didn't
she?

As if she'd caught him staring, she fumbled with her
ring, giving a curt nod. "If you're worried about the
work, well, it *isn't* going to be a small job. And it *will*

be quite a challenge," she said, as though he hadn't spoken. "I've never really undertaken something of this magnitude, but I do know what I'm doing. I can assure you of that, at least."

Jake had the feeling things were getting away from him.

"Ms. Buchanan?" He frowned down at her. "I think we have a problem here."

His frown seemed to have some effect.

For two seconds, maybe three, he saw that slightly startled, slightly nervous look return to her eyes as if eleven years hadn't really drifted by. Then she pulled herself up straighter, turning her head from him. She reached out and stroked her fingers over a bit of wood, examining it as if she'd never seen this house before. As if she needed something to hold on to.

"Yes?" she asked, not looking at him.

"Ms. Buchanan," Jake drawled, trying to snag her complete attention. He gentled his voice. "Darlin', would you mind telling me something, please?"

The lady halted her perusal, her back stiffened. When she turned to look at him, questioningly, Jake noticed the telltale tinge of rose that had climbed to her cheekbones.

He crossed his arms and leaned back against the house as he watched her like a falcon keeping its prey in its sights. "What in the name of Misunderstood are you really doing here, lady? What is it exactly that you want from me?"

As if she'd finally decided to acknowledge the fact that she was standing in a grizzly's path, the lady looked up at him, her eyes wide, hesitant and—apologetic? "I'm…here to help you," she said slowly.

"To help me?"

"Of course. I told you, I'm the chairwoman of the—"

"Historical Preservation Committee," he finished for her. "And you're here to—"

She shook her head impatiently. "To help you restore your mother's home."

"To its former glory," he added, mimicking her earlier words.

"Exactly," she agreed. "I'm the committee's expert on historic renovation. It's a topic I've studied extensively and I have some degree of experience. I've tackled summer projects. Not around here very much, but still…"

Her voice trailed off, and Jake realized that he was glowering at her. Good. She was talking nonsense.

"Lady, I don't know what you're talking about, but I'm not the slightest bit interested in historic renovation. I'm here to do some basic shoring up and that's that. I plan to be in and out of town in a couple of weeks. Tops."

Tess Buchanan's brows arched; she took a deep breath and stared him down. "You said you would do what was necessary, Mr. Walker," she reminded him, and all traces of hesitance faded away. That vulnerable trace of something he'd thought he'd seen in her eyes vanished like smoke in the path of wild wind.

Knowing who she was, Jake had to give her points for gutsiness. Hell, he'd already given her points just for walking across the road to speak to him.

"Maybe we don't agree on what's necessary," he said softly.

"Apparently we don't," she conceded. "And maybe you don't completely understand, Mr. Walker. This house is a Queen Anne, a perfect example of one, I might add, and it's located in a part of the town that burned to the ground in the 1890's and had to be rebuilt. Although it alone has no historic significance, it *is* subject to the rules governing this part of town. Any repairs or reconstruction must be conducted according to the guidelines set up by the committee.''

She paused and waited, chin up, for his reaction to her statement. Her eyes were dark with challenge and pride.

Jake noticed those magnificent eyes, but mostly he noticed that she was suggesting a course of action that would keep him here far longer than he would ever consider staying.

''I don't give a snap of my fingers for the committee's guidelines,'' he said slowly, distinctly.

''Then you don't care if this house is destroyed?''

''Why would you think I cared when you don't even know me?'' he said suddenly, and he knew he was overstepping the line. She either didn't remember who he was, or she thought *he* didn't remember *her*.

Her eyes widened, she took a too-deep breath, but she held her ground. She drew her shoulders back. A fighting stance, he thought with amusement.

''You're here, aren't you?''

A direct hit. Jake almost smiled.

He shook his head, looked to the side. ''They'd tear her house down if I didn't follow their silly guidelines?''

''They wouldn't even let you nail one stick of wood to the structure. Permits,'' she explained, and she didn't apologize.

''And how would you feel if they bulldozed this place?'' He turned again to stare her straight in the eye. ''You seem to be taking an inordinate amount of interest in this house.''

She held his gaze for a few seconds before looking

away. He wondered if she was counting to ten. *He* would have been if he'd had to deal with himself.

"It's my job to be interested," she told him. "Besides—" The lady held out one hand, then let it drop. "You obviously saw—that is, I live right across the road. Of course I want this renovation to be handled properly. This is a beautiful old building that should be treated with loving care. It's a house made for living in."

But it hadn't really been lived in since his mother was a girl. When children had tumbled and run and laughed in this place. Jake remembered how his mother had entertained him with stories of her childhood when he'd been five years old and sick with chicken pox. Before his father had gotten into trouble with the law. He pushed the thought aside impatiently. Old history that no longer mattered.

"Mr. Walker?" she asked when he still hadn't spoken.

Jake took a deep breath and looked right into eyes that were filled with concern.

"Do you have any choice?" she continued.

No, damn it, he didn't. And since leaving this town, he hadn't had to deal with that back-to-the-wall feeling. The world he lived in now was his alone; he'd realized the value of solitude. He'd finished school, then managed to fall into a good career writing technical manuals that offered almost total privacy, a future, plenty of possibility, and little in the way of temptation or trouble. It was the way he wanted things, and the sooner he knuckled under and did what he had to do around here, the sooner he could get back to the comfortable niche he'd carved out for himself.

Jake blew out a breath. He glared at Tess Buchanan.

"Okay, lady, you win. I'll abide by your guidelines if I have to."

Just one corner of Tess's lips rose, revealing a dimple along with a look of pure satisfaction and—relief.

"You won't regret this, Mr. Walker," she told him, lifting her chin in a proud, triumphant gesture. "And you might even find that you enjoy this kind of thing."

Jake suddenly wanted to laugh, to howl like a wolf on a chain. He was already regretting his forced decision. And enjoyment wasn't in the plan. Working next to this lady—this way too innocent, way too attractive, clearly off limits lady—well, he knew now that working with Tess Buchanan was going to be more like torture than enjoyment. He might not be everything that everyone thought he was, but he was sure as hell no saint.

What he was, exactly, was a man, and his working parts were all in order and on red alert right now.

"I'm sure you've got enough enthusiasm for both of us," he assured her, resting one hand on his outthrust hip as he leaned against the house.

She shrugged sheepishly. "Well, maybe, but…your mother would be pleased," she assured him softly. "She was a really sweet lady."

The absolute sincerity of her smile, her words, her tone of voice drifted into Jake's consciousness. What she was saying was no surprise to him. He knew just how deep his mother's sweetness had gone. It had made her vulnerable. Way too vulnerable. And here was another vulnerable woman opening herself up like a flower, an easy target for the wrong kind of person. A shaft of irritation glanced off the shield of stoicism he'd been trying to erect.

He glanced down at her ring pointedly.

"Does your fiancé know that you're going to be working with me?"

A moment of silence, of confusion. "Grayson?" she asked, shaking her head. "Why do you ask?"

Grayson. It wasn't that common a name. Not that common at all. Except he had known one man once upon a time...

"Grayson Alexander, if I remember, was a pretty straight arrow. I'm not sure he'd approve of this arrangement," Jake said.

He hoped to hell the guy wouldn't approve. What man in his right mind would want his lady spending time with a known hell-raiser like himself? What man wouldn't do his best to protect her and try to talk her out of doing something so ill-advised? Maybe if Grayson got involved, he'd pull the plug on this whole scenario. Or at least maybe they'd substitute some other "historical expert," some old, crusty man. That, Jake could live with. Not Tess Buchanan. Seeing her smile, hearing the sad note in her voice when she'd mentioned his mother, watching her breasts rise and fall beneath the folds of her jacket—damn, this *was* impossible.

Uh-oh, he'd made her mad. She was wearing that stern schoolteacher look again.

"Grayson is an adult," she said slowly. "And so am I. We don't direct each other's lives. When we're married, when he runs for mayor this fall, I will, of course, stand by his side. But until that time, we've agreed to live our own lives. Now if you're done interfering in my personal life..."

"The way *you're* interfering in mine?" he asked, reaching back and knocking his hand against the wall of the house. "But then, you made it clear, this is your job. I just thought that given our...personal history, your fiancé might have a problem with you working so closely with me.''

He could see her sucking in air as she pulled herself up. Deep rose invaded her ivory skin. He was making her uncomfortable.

Good.

"Or perhaps you don't remember me?" he asked, knowing now that she did, knowing he was prepared to press his point further if he had to. Anything to get her to walk away from this and send in someone else to do the job.

The lady dragged those shoulders back. She stood tall and stared him dead in the eye. "I guess I *do* remember you after all, Jake Walker," she said. "It's just that— maybe it's the setting. You'd probably look a bit more familiar if you were in a closet surrounded by school supplies—and if your hand was up a woman's dress, of course."

Her face was bright crimson, but she wasn't backing down an inch. She was magnificent, her breath coming hard and fast. He knew that she was about as uncomfortable as a woman could get in these circumstances, but it was apparent that there was no way she was going to let him steamroll her into giving up. He'd thought she might turn and run if he pushed, but she hadn't—just as she hadn't run all those years ago.

Giving in, giving up, he shook his head and gave her a slight smile. "Touché, Tess," he said softly. "I deserved that. You and I both know that you just did what you had to do that day."

She nodded tightly. "And that's what I'm doing now—Jake," she said, nearly stumbling over her words. "Here, with this house—and you. It's what I'll continue to do. What I have to do, what's necessary, what's right.''

"You're pretty tough?" he asked.

"Sometimes it's the only way to be. Remember that when I start issuing orders about this house. I have a tendency to get pretty bossy.''

"And I have a tendency to be pretty stubborn," he admitted.

She ducked her head in agreement. "At least we've cleared the air, and we both know what we're up against. I've got summer students to tutor today, but if you've got time tomorrow, we'll begin to discuss our course of action.''

"We'll talk then," he agreed.

But as she made her way back home, he couldn't have disagreed with her more. They hadn't cleared the air, and she most certainly didn't have a clue about what she was up against.

This lady was a straight shooter, a teacher, for heaven's sake, a pillar of the community engaged to another pillar of the community. Someone who still believed in truth, justice, and the Golden Rule.

Jake groaned at the thought. He remembered all the rules he'd broken in his lifetime, the times he'd failed to tell the truth. Deliberately. No remorse. He wasn't sorry for who and what he was. Never had been. Still there was no escaping the fact that the lady was clearly his opposite in every way. She was also completely un-available—for anything that didn't pertain to this house—but that didn't stop him from studying the way her skirt caressed the curves of her legs as she walked away from him. It damn well didn't stop him from ad-miring the sway of her hips as she moved back to her own side of the road.

Tess Buchanan would be a fool to trust herself to Jake Walker, but she had. So it looked like he was going to have to be the one who exerted some common sense around here.

Too bad he'd always had a deplorable shortage of common sense, especially where women were concerned. And she ought to know that. She really should remember that. If he'd been thinking straight eleven years ago, if he'd acted the way Grayson Alexander would have, he and Tess would never have met at all.

Chapter Two

"That's the third time you've dropped your pencil. You okay, Ms. Buchanan?"

Tess quickly scooped up the errant pencil. She hoped she wasn't blushing as she turned to the young girl who faced her across the table.

"I'm fine, Sally," she said, nodding. "But I think maybe we've covered enough for today. "Your grasp of algebra has improved markedly in the last few weeks. You should be proud of yourself."

Sally ducked her head and smiled, gathering her books and pencils together as she prepared to leave. "Thanks, Ms. Buchanan, and I guess I am a little proud, but if Mr. Davis was half the teacher you are, I would have passed the first time around."

Tess knew she shouldn't feel such an inner glow. She knew she should reprimand Sally, but the truth was that Allen Davis *was* as boring as oatmeal without raisins.

"Just pass this time, Sally," she said with a sigh. "All right?"

The young girl chuckled. "Just watch me, Ms. Buchanan. Just watch."

Sally hitched her backpack over her shoulder and headed for the door. With one hand on the frame, she turned to Tess.

"My mother says you're going to help fix up that place across the street this summer. She told me to tell you to be careful."

Tess caught her breath. She stared at Sally and shrugged.

"I'm always careful, Sally," she said slowly.

"I know, but Mom says—" Sally shut her mouth as Tess drew herself up to her full height and rose from the table, staring at Sally the way she'd stared at hundreds of students who were out of line and who knew it.

"I'll be careful," Tess promised, bending a bit. She really didn't want to hurt Sally's feelings.

The girl tossed her head and grinned, wrinkling her nose. "Heck, I told her there was nothing to worry about. You're too smart to do something stupid even if he does look like heaven on a Harley." She rolled her eyes, nodding toward the door in the direction of Jake's house. "Just because the guy used to have every woman for miles panting after him doesn't mean spit to someone like you. You're different. Besides, you're engaged to Mr. Alexander. You wouldn't be interested. I *told* Mom that. Don't be mad at us."

Tess shook her head. She smiled. "I wasn't mad, Sally, just startled, that's all. You just keep studying that algebra, okay? I'll see you next week."

But after Sally had gone, Tess had to admit that she hadn't been entirely truthful with the girl. She *had* been less than careful yesterday. She'd been caught off guard several times. She'd been so relieved when Jake had given in and agreed to go along with the committee's guidelines without argument, that she'd found herself falling under the spell of those deep green eyes. Her heart had tripped along far too fast, and she hadn't been able to help but smile at the man.

Of course her pleasure had simply been because of the house. She'd always loved that place and had even shared an occasional impersonal conversation with the sweet-eyed woman who'd once lived there. Flora Walker had been devoted to her house and her garden—and it pleased Tess no end to realize she herself was finally going to be able to help bring the place back to life. Of course that sudden joy was bound to mess with her mind a little.

That was why she'd been a bit clumsy today. It had nothing to do with the man who lived there. He might have killer eyes and a body that conjured up visions of hot summer nights and naked flesh, but she'd gotten her misplaced hurt feelings and her Jake Walker fantasies out of her system years ago. And she wasn't one to subscribe to the popular belief that because the man had once been a kid caught in the act in a school setting, he was an animal waiting to pounce.

Indeed, after years of teaching, Tess knew enough about youthful hormones to wonder why she didn't find more teenagers sneaking around between the reams of construction paper and piles of old textbooks. She'd gotten past his indiscretion. What she couldn't dismiss was Jake's treatment of Cassie afterward, the fact that he'd tossed her aside like discarded laundry.

Tess knew about those kinds of things, too. Men with a certain appeal, but no honor. Her father had carried on for years as though he wasn't even married; her own husband had left her when she was still recovering from an auto accident. So she'd meant what she said when she'd told Sally she'd be careful.

She'd be darned certain she didn't touch him again. That handshake had been a mistake, and she wasn't a woman who made mistakes often—or who had any desire to walk on the wild side. In Grayson she had all the qualities she admired in a man: kindness, loyalty, respect. He knew, of course, about her and Jake and agreed that eleven-year-old incidents were best forgotten. She intended to do just that—and to ignore the man across the road, as well.

Today she was past the initial meeting, the inevitable awkwardness of admitting her past connection to Jake Walker. From here on out she could concentrate completely on the house.

Tess came dressed more casually today, Jake noticed—but she was still carrying a book and a fussy little clipboard that somehow suited her. She set the book down, but held tightly to the clipboard, tucked it in close against her chest, almost a protective gesture, and her smile was determined and careful. He knew what she was doing, pretending he wasn't who he was, and he also knew that he ought to be glad and grateful. Her approach should have made things simpler and less personal, but that uncertain smile of hers. Darn, but it was deadly.

"Good morning," she said, deepening the smile just a shade. The effect was automatic. Jake almost had to slap himself to convince himself that she hadn't said, "Come to bed, Jake."

Say good morning to the lady, Jake, he told himself, and he did so without any smile of welcome.

There was no denying that Tess attracted him—and

that fact bugged the heck out of him. She was a woman with a firm commitment to this town. She was the type who embraced responsibility and causes and, obviously, good old Grayson Alexander, while he—hell, all he wanted to embrace was the notion of saving and selling his mother's home as quickly as possible so he could make tracks back to his private retreat in California.

Over. Done. Simple.

Still, staring down at the beauty in front of him, Jake knew as sure as he was breathing too hard that there was not going to be anything simple about this whole operation—unless he took it upon himself to personally see to it that Tess didn't smile at him too much or too often. It had been a while since he'd met a woman who could seduce him with a simple smile, and he wasn't sure how trustworthy he could be in the face of such temptation. Time to let the lady know just what and who she was dealing with.

"Eager to begin the next phase of our…relationship, Tess?" He motioned toward the newborn sun. "It's early."

She paused slightly, her smile frozen. "Not exactly, Mr. Walker. I'd say I'm just a morning person. But then, apparently so are you."

Jake raised the corner of his lips. "Maybe. Or maybe I just had activities that kept me up all night."

He wasn't lying about that. He'd been cruising toward completion of a book on computer hardware and had stayed up to finish it, but the truth might make her soften with sympathy. He couldn't have that.

"I could use a bit of time in bed right now," he admitted with a tired grin.

For a fraction of a second her violet eyes registered panic, the desire to walk back out that door. Then she crossed her arms slowly and stared him down. "Well, I guess I'll just have to pinch you if you doze off. We've got work to do, Mr. Walker."

God, the lady had guts. He was doing his best to get under her skin, to keep her waltzing backward so there'd be some breathing space between them, but she wasn't about to let him get the upper hand.

Her eyes might say babe-in-the-woods, but she was going to do her damnedest to make him be the one to cry "uncle."

That was okay. If she was giving him prim little lectures, she wouldn't be smiling up at him and making him forget that there were good reasons to keep his distance from her.

Of course, forcing Tess to the wall was a double-edged sword. She looked seductive as hell when she stood her ground. But at least he'd created some distance. He could feast his eyes on her without worrying about his hands misbehaving.

Slowly, Jake formed his lips into a broad smile and raised his brows at the lady who was still waiting for his reaction to her comment. "Go ahead and pinch me if you want to, Tess. I promise to stand still while you do."

He'd gone overboard on that one. He'd expected her to get her back up. He'd expected her to try to shoot him down. What he hadn't expected was her sudden pallor, the sharp intake of breath, that suddenly repentant look.

"I—oh, heck, I thought we settled things yesterday," she said softly, "but of course that was foolish and naive of me. Of course you're still angry at me and I can understand that. You and Cassie may have made a mistake that day, but believe me, I never wanted you to be expelled. I've always wished I'd been older and more experienced, brave enough to speak up in your defense, or at least that I'd closed the door before anyone else arrived..."

She faltered, the apology clear in her voice and Jake found himself taking a dangerous step closer.

"You think— Damn, you think I blame you for that day? That any of that was your fault?"

"It was my answers to the superintendent's questions that sealed your fate."

Jake shook his head in wonder and disbelief. "That's rich. You don't know how many times I'd sat in the principal's office before that. The chair was probably still sizzling from the last time I'd been there. My poor mother spent more time coming to the school than she did tending to her own home. Besides, *I* was the one in that closet, Tess. It was my stupidity that did me in. How could I blame you for simply being honest?"

She was still looking guilty. She opened her mouth, then closed it again.

"It wasn't your fault—or Cassie's, either," he said firmly.

And that *was* the truth. Tess had done nothing wrong, and Cassie might have pulled at his clothes and twined herself around him, but he knew now that she hadn't been thinking clearly that day. She'd been frightened out of her wits when she'd led him into that closet. She'd been desperately unhappy and in need of someone she knew and trusted to hold her and reassure her, to restore the sense of self that she'd temporarily lost. And anyway, *he* was the one who'd followed a pale, trembling Cassie when he'd known that even the illusion of wrong-doing would damage any future he had left at the school, when he knew just how desperately his mother wanted to see him finish high school. He'd always walked a thin line in this town, but when his sometime ally had clung to him in that closet, he hadn't pushed her away. He'd held her and tried to figure out what was going on. He'd taken his chances, taken a fall, and ended up right where everyone always thought he would. But it had been his own choice to do so.

Jake looked down and saw that Tess was smiling at him again. Damn.

"I hear that Cassie moved to Hightower," she offered slowly, tentatively. "She...she had a child."

Jake took a deep breath. He knew what he was supposed to say here. She was hoping he'd be surprised. The Pollyanna in her wanted all the men in her world to be squeaky-clean and roam around on antiseptic white horses doing good deeds. She wanted him to turn the past around and tell her that everything she'd inevitably heard about him was just a bunch of lies. It would make this time with him more acceptable, easier. She wanted him to reassure her.

Instead he stared her dead in the eye. "I know Cassie had a baby," he said simply. "I heard about that."

He *had* heard, finally, and he knew the story—more of it than most did—but that was nobody's business but his and Cassie's. He had secrets to keep and they weren't his alone. The truth was not to be told. Especially not to this woman. She believed in the power of total honesty, but for poverty-stricken kids like Cassie had been or for sons of ex-cons like himself, truth didn't always come in a pretty package. It was definitely not for every situation.

Tess looked up at Jake. She waited for him to say more, to tell her that he hadn't heartlessly left the mother of his child to fend for herself, but he simply stared back at her, his eyes as full of challenge as they'd ever been eleven years ago.

"Well, I—I suppose we'd better get down to business," she said, trying to shrug off the ridiculous sense of disappointment she felt. What had she expected, anyway? Just because the man took the blame for getting himself and Cassie expelled? Because he'd looked at her with understanding in his eyes? So what if she'd felt an achingly awful need to touch him and absolve him of all guilt?

Nonsense. Daydreams. Of course. The man looked, as everyone said, like heaven, and naturally she'd want him to act that way, too. It was perfectly understandable that she'd fantasize a bit. Who wouldn't? But—

She cleared her throat as he continued to study her.

"Business," he agreed, holding one hand out in a sweep of the room. "My castle, fair lady," he said, nodding toward the whole disastrous interior with a wicked grin.

The room was both beautiful and awful. Torn expanses of wallpaper that had at one time been a lovely and bold floral design were now faded and spotted in places where the roof had leaked. The squares of period paneling were cracked in places. Once golden solid wood floors were horribly warped while sunlight streamed in through a fanlight window in a delicate patterned dance that emphasized dust, deterioration, and the dying splendor of another time.

"Like it?" he asked.

Tess rolled her eyes. "I've been here before," she assured him.

"They do that, do they? The committee comes in when people aren't home to look around?"

His voice was even, casual. She'd bet he was angry

as ten demons in a paper bag. And why not, considering what he was thinking?

"Of course not. There are laws, you know, Walker."

"So—"

"So your mother invited me in for coffee once. I guess I looked so pathetically interested in this place that she decided to satisfy my curiosity. It was already beginning to look pretty bad then."

What was that look that flitted across Jake's face? A wince?

Probably not. More wishful thinking on her part.

He nodded tersely. "I have the papers that explain what needs to be done."

She stepped closer, sure he wasn't going to like what she was going to tell him next. "I know. There are roof repairs, electrical work, window replacements, the damage to the basic structure, things that are needed to bring the building up to code. But some of those have to be handled with great care. Research has to be done. The paint for instance—"

"Something as simple as paint is going to be a problem, is it?" Jake's voice was a deep challenge. She could hear the hint of stubbornness that he'd told her about. "So what do I need to know about—paint?"

The man made something as innocuous as wall color sound like a curse—or a sexual exercise. Tess felt her face heating, but she'd be damned if she was going to let this stubborn man get the better of her. She loved this house, she was sure the woman who'd lived in it had loved it, too, and she was darn well going to see that Jake Walker did right by the place. His reluctance was understandable. It couldn't be pleasant staying in a town where everyone saw him as the bogeyman, but this home had been his mother's. He had cared for her.

There'd been that reluctant catch in his throat when he'd mentioned Flora yesterday. And maybe it wasn't nice, or even proper, but Tess intended to bank on Jake Walker's affection for his mother.

Like it or not, she and Jake were going to be fairly tight for a while. She had the feeling she was going to have to fight him for every little thing, every extra minute of investment in this house she got.

"Well, Jake, there's paint and then there's—paint," she whispered, tossing her head, knowing he'd recognize that she was going to go head-to-head with him at his own game. She wanted him to know that, to see that she wouldn't be cowed by some big hunk of a man just because he tried to scare her off with a few suggestive comments.

"I guess I just never realized," Jake conceded on a drawl. He raised one brow, tilting his head in acknowledgment of her counterattack.

"Yes," she continued, handing him the book she'd brought with her. "Here's some background information for you. You'll find that the Victorian range of color was a bit more limited than what we're used to today. Browns, reds and greens were quite popular, but Queen Annes—"

"I was thinking of electric blue and purple, darlin'," he said, interrupting her, and she could see that he was working to suppress a grin.

"Interesting," she said, crossing her arms and raising one brow the way she frequently did when a student tried to put her on. The man was trying to bait her, probably trying to get her to back off and back down, but she was not going to be baited.

"Just a guess, but are you trying to be difficult, Walker?" she asked, coming straight to the point.

He shrugged. "Maybe it just comes naturally to some of us."

She'd just bet it did. His low, lazy drawl sent little whispers of sensation swirling down through her body, making her clothes feel uncomfortably tight in a way that she didn't want them to. She couldn't feel that way about Jake Walker. No way.

Because of Grayson, but also because of Jake himself. The man was a whirling bundle of contradiction, and she didn't want to get too close. He'd bluntly admitted that he'd left a young girl to face the shame and humiliation of bearing his child while he'd been far away, then passionately defended Cassie. He'd abandoned his mother, but obviously had loved the woman. He had reason to resent Tess herself, but had vehemently absolved her of all guilt. And in the next breath, he did his best to warn her away.

She stared at him unblinkingly.

He grinned back, still silent and waiting for her to make her next move.

Jake Walker was a mystery, walls within walls, trouble of the worst kind. He was a man who didn't seem to know what he wanted, and she'd had her fill of that kind.

On the other hand, he also reminded her of a male student she'd once taught—a kid who'd tried to intimidate her into letting him fail—and that was a useful bit of knowledge.

She'd nearly lost that battle with her student. Nearly, but not quite. And so she did now the only thing she could think of to do, the one thing that had always worked for her in the past. She ignored all of Jake's mysterious past and concentrated on the man in front of her now. She willed herself to do her best to break down the barriers to their working relationship, such as it was.

She smiled and pretended that he wasn't being a bear.

"I'm sorry to hear that being difficult comes naturally to you, Jake, but we still have business to conduct together."

The man glowered. He muttered a low and distinct curse, and she could swear she heard the words "nosy, interfering woman."

Tess held her smile.

"Would you stop doing that?" he demanded.

Tilting her head, Tess raised one brow. "Doing what?"

"Stop being so damn nice when I've just practically insulted you."

Thrusting her chin up, Tess stared at him dead-on. "No, you didn't *just practically* insult me, Jake. You've *pointedly* insulted me several times already this morning. But I figure that at least one of us has to be nice if we're going to work together. And we are going to work together, aren't we?" She glanced down at the paper that listed the repairs that had to be made if the house was not to be condemned and then turned back to Jake. She raised her brows, like a wistful kid awaiting a parent's uncertain verdict.

Jake looked at the earnest expression in Tess's eyes, the determined thrust of that delicate chin. And he couldn't help it; he shook his head and smiled back at her.

"Lady, you have got to be one of most up-front women that I've ever met. Have you always gotten your way this easily?"

She took a shaky and visible breath, as if he'd startled

her into thinking about things she didn't want to remember.

"Of course not," she conceded softly. "But then, this one's easy. You don't have much choice, do you?"

"You know I don't. But—"

The lady stood there silent, waiting.

"I want this to be fast and over with quickly," he said, leveling with her. "If I'm being a pain, well…" He held out his hands, palm up in dismissal. "I can't stay here that long, but you're talking research and that always means time." It did, in his line of work, anyway.

Tess nodded, her shoulders visibly relaxed. "Well, then, don't worry, Walker. It won't mean much time in this case. I know my time periods, I've specialized in Victorians. If you want to speed things along, I can draw up a list of suggestions, choices for you to make that will simplify matters."

Finally, they were seeing eye to eye.

"But just remember something, Jake," she said, and Jake was astonished to see the lady step closer, close enough for him to reach out and touch her. "I know that you care more about this house than you're letting on. I don't know what the exact situation was between you and your mother, but I suspect that you did care about her and that you'd want her to be proud and happy about the end results of this project. I won't go easy on you. This *isn't* going to be a slap of paint here, a nail or two there. This is going to be a labor of love. I hope you understand that I have to give this my all."

Jake looked down into those violet eyes. He surveyed the satiny shining crown of her hair, the soft curve of her lips.

She was a delicate woman, sweet forbidden fruit. She wanted something good for this town, something good in his mother's name. She *was* a good woman—and she belonged to Grayson Alexander, a man who no doubt deserved every delicious inch of her.

And *he* was Jake Walker, a man whose name had once brought a groan of distress to the hearts of every mother of every young woman in town.

It was important for him to remember all of that—and that Tess be aware of the state of things, too.

Slowly, deliberately, he cupped his palm around her jaw. He dragged his thumb over the fullness of her lower lip.

"I understand that you'll always have to do what you think is right, Tess," he said, his voice low and intimate. "But you understand one thing about me. Don't try to psychoanalyze me into being something I never was or want to be. Don't forget just who I am."

He slid his thumb back over her lip the other way, a slow caress filled with meaning. A warning.

Within his hand, he felt her tremble. He was close enough to note that her breathing had deepened even as his own had. Her pupils dilated, her lids fluttered, but then she caught herself. She stared back at him as she reached up and removed his hand, folding her own hand around it as she stepped away.

She turned his touch into a handshake.

"Jake, just because I like to get things done as pleasantly as possible, just because I don't blame you and Cassie for your youthful indiscretion, doesn't mean I've forgotten what happened," she said carefully. "I'm not likely to *ever* forget that Cassie is somewhere, raising a child without a husband to help her. And I'm not likely to forget who *I* am or what I want, either," she continued, pulling her hand away from his as she adjusted the engagement ring on her finger.

Without adding another word, she turned and moved off toward the door. With a squeak of hinges, she pulled it back, stopping to look at him once more.

"I'm going to go home and work like crazy to draw up some ideas for you. Be prepared to be cooperative. You're going to have a full day of me the next time, Jake, and we're going to make some important decisions. We're going to do this right."

The slamming door bounced back and forth a few times as she walked away with a quick snap of her heels against the porch slats. Jake watched her hurried stride as she descended the stairs and crossed the road. He seemed to be spending a whole lot of time watching the woman walk away from him.

And a whole lot more time trying to keep her out of his mind.

A full day.

Damn. Jake bit down on a groan.

He knew what *he* would have. A full night of tossing and turning and trying to forget what it had felt like to touch her.

He had known he hadn't wanted to come back to Misunderstood. Now he knew exactly why.

And things became even clearer at two in the morning. The clicking of rain on the window woke Jake. Groggy, he heard the soft thud of droplets falling on the pillow next to his.

He reached over—to draw Tess next to him, to pull her safely into the protection of his arms and rescue her from the threat of any discomfort.

Soft violet eyes smiled back at him in his mind—but his arms remained empty. The remnants of the dream Tess dissolved. Vanished. Immediately.

Jake groaned, sat up, wiped his palm across his jaw.

He finished three more chapters in the hours before dawn—but that wasn't important. The important thing was that he was able to keep his thoughts of Tess at bay.

Jake figured he was going to write a lot of books in the next few weeks. He was going to make a lot of money.

He was going to lose a hell of a lot of sleep.

Chapter Three

Standing on Jake's front steps two days later, Tess took deep breaths to prepare herself. She'd been up for two nights straight, poring over paperwork and plans.

She'd been doing her best to forget Jake's drugging caress of her lips.

And she'd spent an awful lot of time trying to evade her memories of Jake with his hand up Cassie's dress.

The very thought made her squirm. It was a vision that crept in at the most aggravating moments when she was tired from overwork. And having experienced the slow stroke of Jake's touch herself only made things worse. She could all too easily understand how Cassie had ended up in that closet. Against her will, Tess could almost envision how his long, strong fingers would feel against her own thigh.

She sucked in a deep breath as the thought slipped in.

Damn the man. She knew that he'd touched her because she'd been getting carried away with her enthusiasm for this project. He'd meant to warn her that he was not safe or trustworthy like Grayson was.

But she'd already known that. She'd known that he was a man who didn't play by the rules. Reality would have knocked on her door in time. She hadn't needed that touch to realize the truth. She wished he hadn't whisked his thumb against her lips and made them burn. It would only make working with him more difficult.

But it would also spur her to be as speedy as he wished.

The man was devious—and obviously effective at getting his way.

She would hurry about her business.

And she would darn well not think about Jake's hand—anywhere—again. It was disloyal to Grayson to do so, and if there was one thing Tess valued, it was loyalty.

Tess let go of the spindlework porch support as she squared her shoulders in determination and stepped over the missing slat in the floor.

She stared at the closed door. This was the first visit she'd made here when Jake hadn't met her at the door or on the porch. She braced herself, took a firmer grasp on the briefcase she carried, and banged on the door.

No answer.

Tess knocked again.

Still no answer.

Should she go back home and call? Would the man even have a phone yet? What if he was upstairs or in the back of the house and simply couldn't hear her pounding?

"Jake?"

Still no answer.

She called his name again.

Tess looked around, realizing that she was standing in the open in broad daylight, bellowing for the most notorious man in town to come and let her into his house.

There was something almost obscene about the situation—or maybe something comical.

The corners of her lips tilted up as she thought of how absurd she must appear standing out here trying not to yell too loudly. Shaking her head, Tess gave a shrug as she turned to go home. Obviously Jake wasn't here.

Maybe he'd changed his mind and left town again.

The thought made her mind lurch crazily for a second. Of course, there was a good reason for that dizzy, uncomfortable feeling. She wanted to restore this place to the fairy-tale house Flora had remembered with love. And she needed Jake for that. That was all.

When the house was done, she would be glad for him to go. More than glad. Then she could get back to her easy, comfortable life with Grayson that had been interrupted by the last few days' work.

But as Tess's toes brushed the grassy area in front of Jake's house, the roar of an engine made her look up.

Jake rolled toward her, stopped his motorcycle in the drive and removed his helmet. His long black hair was slightly mussed, his eyes were lit with amusement as he easily climbed off the cycle and walked toward her with that slow, rolling gait.

There was absolutely nothing easy or comfortable about Jake Walker. Tess automatically raised her chin when he neared her.

"I'd given up on you," he said, glancing up at the noontime sun. "This is awfully late for you, Ms. Buchanan. No sunrise rendezvous this morning?"

She ignored the heat she felt creeping up from the collar of her blouse. "I thought maybe I'd wait until you'd had your nap for the day." Which was a lie. The truth was that she'd decided that Jake at dawn was just too deadly. She wanted to face him in the dream-banishing light of day this time.

"That was thoughtful of you," he agreed with a grin. "But I don't nap unless I've got good reason to be tired."

Tess could just bet he had good reason pretty often as she tried not to notice how his black T-shirt stretched taut across his chest.

She dropped her gaze to the bundle he was carrying. The stamp of the Misunderstood Public Library edged on the books was clearly visible.

"You're interested in using recycled materials?" She peered at the books and immediately regretted the incredulous note in her voice. As a teacher she considered it her life's task to encourage, not make anyone feel self-conscious about their interests. She was out of line.

Jake watched as Tess's cheeks turned a delightful pink. He raised his eyebrows, let his smile broaden.

"I've given up my days of throwing half-smoked cigarette butts on the ground just to be cool," he said, trying to ruffle her feathers a bit, even though the books were, in reality, the beginnings of research for his next project.

Tess opened her eyes wide at his comment, the slight lift of her lips bringing a dimple out of hiding. "Was that really considered cool?" Her voice was husky with disbelief.

Jake slowly crossed his heart, watching her as he did so. "Yeah. Didn't make much sense, did it?"

She was still smiling as she shook her head. "Kids do a lot of impulsive things that don't make any sense to adults, but those rituals are an important part of a young life. You don't...still smoke?''

He held out his hands in mock surrender. ''Gave it up four years ago.'' His mother had just fallen ill and had been staying in a nursing home. Smoking hadn't been practical.

Tess's brows raised in an approving gesture. ''Lucky man. I guess you get to escape my schoolteacher talk about the dangers of smoking. I don't have to give it often. Most of my students know the score.''

''Ah, a new generation,'' he agreed.

''Different impulses,'' she said. ''Tattoos are very big right now. I wonder how they'll feel about *them* ten years down the road.''

At her words, Jake shifted uncomfortably. ''Is this the beginning of a lecture?''

Tess looked up into his eyes. Her color heightened, bloomed a deep rose. ''The dragon,'' she said softly.

Stupid, he thought. She hadn't seen it yesterday, it was small, on his shoulder, out of sight most of the time— but she *had* seen it once before.

It had been ten kinds of dumb to remind her when she'd already proven to him that she was carrying around a lot of unnecessary guilt concerning that day.

If he'd been the kind of man to redden up, *he'd* be the one blushing right now, Jake was sure.

''Damn, you'd forgotten. I didn't mean to bring it up.''

Tess held up one hand to stop him. ''I hadn't forgotten, I just...well, it *is* small,'' she said primly, sticking to the subject. ''And private. Just for your eyes and for your...well, that is, it's really no one's business but yours, is it? And...I'm glad to hear that you don't smoke anymore. Cigarettes and old houses don't make especially good partners.''

The lady was a trouper. She had taken his comment and tossed it away as unimportant, even though he was sure that the subject was still uncomfortable for her. He still made her uncomfortable. And why not? She'd fallen into the belief that he would abandon an innocent girl in trouble as easily as everyone else had, no questions asked, and he'd done nothing to change that. Why else was she totally buttoned down and covered up today in an oversize jacket and a pair of loose slacks, her only concession to femininity the lacy little butterflies at her ears? Why else was she wearing something that hid every curve she owned and made her look—utterly adorable, lost in her big clothes with her big violet eyes that did unbelievably erotic things to his insides. And why shouldn't she be uncomfortable and cautious, believing what she did about him?

Jake cleared his throat, he wished the denim of his jeans had more give in the groin area.

He tried a plastic grin. ''I guess that's your way of reminding me to get my butt inside and get to work? Okay, let's do it, Tess. I promised you cooperation. You promised me speed and efficiency. Come on in and hit me with your game plan.''

And Tess did just that.

For the next few hours she led Jake upstairs, downstairs, inside and outside. She pointed out what things he *had* to do and what choices he could make. They discussed the probable cost of repairing a steeply hipped roof that had a cross gable. They talked about the types of decorative shingles that might have been removed from the gable and replaced with plain clapboard.

''Of course,'' Tess said, rushing on, ''I realize that

you'll need to separate the want-to's from the have-to's. Restoration can be quite expensive. I don't mean to get personal but..." She hesitated, looked at a spot somewhere about three inches to the left of his ear, Jake estimated. "We'll need to discuss cost in more detail. You'll need to tell me whether you can afford..."

She was coloring up just beautifully again. Jake reached out and passed his hand in front of her face to get her complete attention. He smiled and decided to let her off the hook.

"I'm gainfully employed," he told her, grinning wider as she appeared to let out her breath. He wondered if she'd pictured him riding the rails and carrying his worldly belongings on a stick.

"Of course," she said, pushing her hand back over her cheek and through her hair as though to wipe away the telltale blush. "I didn't mean to imply otherwise, but still, *everyone* has their limits. That is, I think we might just concentrate on the basics inside and turn most of our attention to the exterior work. You can deal with things like wallpaper and new plasterwork down the road."

He wouldn't be here down the road, someone else would make those choices, but there was no need to get into all of that now.

"I'll make some decisions tonight," he promised as they made their way through the second floor. He was leading her through one of several guest bedrooms when Tess stopped dead still.

"What's that?" she asked, motioning to the computer on an ancient desk.

Jake tilted his head. He took her hand and led her nearer. "Twentieth-century technology?" he said.

She frowned at him, her eyebrows bunching together

as she reached down and scooped up a book, one on small-appliance repair that he'd written several years earlier.

"You write books?"

Her words came out sounding more like, "You rob banks?"

Jake shrugged. "Hey, it pays the rent—and it's not the kind of job where you have to have a sterling résumé, okay?"

"Jake Walker," Tess said, stepping right up into his face. "I was not questioning your choice of occupation—or trying to pry. I just, well, you never said. No one ever told me."

He chuckled and felt a tightening in his gut as she slicked her hand over the cover of his book. "You write."

She said it with awe, with reverence. She'd said that no one had ever told her. No surprise. They didn't review technical manuals in the Misunderstood *News,* or many other places, for that matter. Not usually, that is.

But she was still stroking her way through the pages, caressing them with a teacher's love for the written word.

Jake wondered what it would feel like to have her delicate fingertips sliding against his skin. He wondered if it were possible for the top of a man's head to blow off from the simple buildup of pure sexual frustration.

"Hey, I'm not Stephen King," he said, reaching out and taking the book from her. "It's just a living, Tess. It suits the kind of solitary life-style I favor."

She was staring at the book like a kid who'd had a toy ripped from her fingers. He wanted to slap himself the way many other women had wanted to slap him over the years.

"You had these kinds of aspirations and you didn't even get to finish high school," she was saying.

"Wrong. I finished high school, just not here," he corrected. "I got my G.E.D., even took some college courses, so don't you dare start beating up on yourself again. It was my damn fault I didn't graduate. I was the one who robbed my mother of the chance to see me get my diploma with everyone else, the one thing she wanted above all others. I knew what I was doing in that closet, Tess. You said you wouldn't forget."

"I haven't," she promised. "I'll never, ever forget that, and I won't forgive you for it, either, but this is so—"

"Materialistic," he said, emphasizing each syllable. "I do it for money, I get paid. Okay?" He tossed the book back on the table.

"Okay," she agreed. "I'm sorry I pried."

"No harm done."

But that wasn't really true. This pathway was dangerous. With her soul-deep love for learning, she might easily make more of his writing than there was. She might begin to think that he was something that he wasn't. And while he hadn't done everything he'd been accused of doing during his years in this town, he'd done plenty. Plenty she didn't even know about.

Besides, even if he hadn't impregnated Cassie, the rap belonged to him. Letting people think he'd abandoned her was better than having everyone say she'd slept around, which was what would happen if he denied his paternity. Hey, there was a kid involved here, one who had enough problems without his mother's reputation being painted black. So to hell with the truth. The truth wouldn't do that kid one bit of good.

"Come on, it's late," he said softly, coaxing her away from his work area. "You must be tired."

She looked up into his eyes, then toward the window where the blue-gray streaks of clouds covered the setting sun. Dark was settling in for the night.

"Yes, you're right, of course. I didn't realize so much time had passed," she said, moving immediately out into the hall and down the stairs.

Jake followed her, watched as her hair swayed with her movements. Two stairs behind her, he noticed how the silken strands separated, falling forward to expose the nape of her neck again and again in a teasing game of peek-a-boo. Pale, vulnerable skin, untouched by the sun, it called for the press of a man's lips.

Stifling his groan, Jake gritted his teeth. So what if he'd managed to pull himself out of the mud, write a few books, and make a simple living? He was never going to be the boy next door or even a distant cousin to the boy next door. That was too damn obvious when every time he got too close to Tess, he wanted to unwrap her like a package and feast his eyes on what was underneath. He had to fight to remember that she was an engaged woman—and even then, he still wanted her. Beneath him. On a bed. In a closet. Just once and only once. So much for his pretense at clean living.

Jake blew out a deep breath as he followed Tess.

She made it to the bottom of the steps, turned around as he joined her and casually braced one shoulder against the wall.

"As soon as you've made your choices, we'll begin setting things in motion." She looked up at him, all business, but that tiny tilt of her softly curved lips, those eyes, made him think of...pleasure. Sweet, shivering pleasure.

He nodded tightly as she turned to leave him behind and head for her home.

"It's getting dark, Tess," he said, pushing off the wall and moving ahead to open the door for her. "Come on, I'll walk you home."

Folding her hand in his own, he moved toward the edge of the stairs and stepped down the short distance to the ground.

"I—"

Jake turned to look up at Tess who was still standing two steps above him on the porch, their hands connecting them.

"It's just across the street." She shook her head and smiling at him uncertainly. "This is Misunderstood."

Jake held on to her hand; he resisted the awful urge to rake his thumb across her palm.

She was right. Of course she was right.

"It would have made my mother happy to think I was acting like a gentleman," he said, grinning up at her. And that was the truth, as well.

Tess answered with a mock-stern look followed by a smile of submission.

"You don't fight fair, Jake Walker," she declared as she moved down to his side and slowly turned toward her house.

"Are we fighting, Ms. Buchanan?" he teased. "I thought I was just walking you home in the dark."

But as his words fell into silence, Jake felt Tess's slight and nearly silent gasp. She wriggled her fingers against his own, tugging on her hand.

Across the road, his hips resting against a sleek white Lexus, was a handsome, chestnut-haired man with watchful eyes.

Instantly Jake released Tess's hand. He felt the cool

air where her fingers had touched his skin and warmed it. He watched as she walked across the road and into the arms of the man she was going to marry.

The road had never seemed so wide, time had never passed so slowly, Tess thought, placing one foot in front of the other as she neared Grayson.

His smile of welcome had never seemed so warm.

"Hi, sunshine. We've got dinner with the Andersons tonight. Remember?"

Tess closed her eyes. She hadn't. Her mind had been too much on—the house. "Oh, Grayson, I'm sorry," she said, walking into his welcoming embrace. "Am I late? Give me ten minutes to change. I'll be right there."

Grayson raised his brows. "So you're not inviting me inside?"

Tess hesitated, feeling her face flush. "Of course," she said, refusing to turn around to see if Jake had gone into his house. "Of course I'm inviting you in."

He smiled and laughed, looping an arm around her neck and scooting her along toward the house. "How are things going with Jake?" he asked once they were inside.

Tess carefully placed her briefcase on her desk. "Good," she finally said with a nod. "He's going to go over my suggestions tonight."

"I'm glad, then. I was a little worried. For your sake."

Tess turned to see that Grayson's golden brown eyes were filled with concern.

"Why?" The word sounded like a bullet smacking against wood. It felt like an accusation.

"Hey, whoa, Tess." Grayson laughed, moving to her and resting his forehead against hers. "I just meant that

I knew that this project meant so much to you. I was afraid he would give you—trouble.''

Tess felt foolish for her near outburst. "You're right. This house *does* mean a lot to me, Grayson. You know I've always admired it. But *you're* on the committee, too.''

He shrugged. "It's not the same. I'm interested in the town as a whole. This house means more to you than that. And Jake...''

His words died away; he held out his hands.

"Is cooperating,'' she said, feeling a small snag of irritation at Grayson's implication.

"He was going to walk you home, wasn't he?''

Tess's hand tingled at Grayson's words, as if an invisible Jake was still standing there, still connected to her. She had to force her mind back to the conversation at hand, to the man beside her, to keep from staring at her palm to see if her hand was still her own.

"Tess?''

"It was getting dark,'' she explained.

Grayson shook his head. "That's not like Jake,'' he said, reminding her of the rumors she'd heard when she first came to town that he and Jake had always been like two opposing warriors poised for battle. "Be careful, Tess.''

His words irritated somehow. She found herself wanting to defend the man across the way.

Instead she looked straight into Grayson's eyes. His concern was genuine. He was worried for her.

"I'm always careful,'' she reminded him.

"I know, and you're a strong, capable woman, but—'' He shrugged, took her hands in his own, thumbed the ring he'd given her. "You can't blame a man for fussing a bit about the woman who's agreed to share her life with him.''

Tess waited for the little lift she always felt when she thought of her future as Mrs. Grayson Alexander. She was not in love with him, nor he with her, but this marriage would be good for both of them. They were the best of friends. He was a kind man who would soon be mayor and would need a wife. She wanted and needed the absolute security he offered. And while his strong good looks and his kisses didn't make her dizzy with want the way all the women in town seemed to think they should, Tess had been exquisitely happy when Grayson had asked her to marry him. Now she went silent, trying to find that feeling again, but her thoughts were interrupted by his quick hug.

"Better get ready or we're going to be late. I'm sorry I questioned you. It's just that Jake—he's hurt people,'' Grayson finished.

"He won't hurt me,'' Tess promised. *And I won't hurt you,* she wanted to add. Instead she went upstairs to get ready for their dinner with the Andersons.

Three hours later when Grayson brought her home and kissed her good-night, she almost couldn't stop herself from repeating that promise again.

I won't hurt you, Grayson. She would never treat this warm, wonderful man the way her father had treated her mother, the way her husband had treated *her.*

Pushing herself deeper into Grayson's arms, Tess sought her place, the reassuring security that this man offered.

But as he said goodbye and drove away into the night, Tess couldn't help noticing that there was a light shining from the second story of Jake's house.

She felt her lips begin to burn—and she rubbed at them with her fingertips.

"I won't hurt you," she whispered to the man who was already gone. It was a promise she intended to keep no matter what.

Chapter Four

He was looking at Tess's *house*, not waiting for the lady herself to step foot outside her door, Jake told himself, standing at his front window, staring out across the street.

He wasn't imagining her soft, slender body in Gray Alexander's arms or imagining what had taken place when she'd disappeared behind those closed doors with her fiancé last night.

None of his business, was it? Nothing he should even be thinking about at all. No way. Not ever.

This house was all he had to worry about, all he was here for. Still, there was no denying the uneasy feeling that passed over him as he noted the definite lean to the tree in Tess's yard. He couldn't completely ignore the way those gnarled branches extended out over the slope of her roof.

Dangerous. Like his own thoughts of Tess.

"Hell." Jake shook his head to shake away the thought. There was no way he should be noticing Tess's tree, her house, or anything else about her. What happened across the street was strictly Tess's concern. She was simply here to do a job, she was here to help him, and she was definitely a part of Grayson Alexander's territory, not Jake Walker's.

Gray Alexander, the man who was going to be mayor of this town, just like he'd once been class president, straight-A student. A near perfect man, an admirable man...and absolutely right for a woman like Tess.

He and Jake had always circled each other warily. They'd even locked horns once, had engaged in an ugly, unresolved battle with fists flying. But that wasn't going to happen this time, Jake thought. He didn't let himself get caught up in fights anymore. It wasn't worth the trouble, and besides, there really wasn't anything to fight over this time. Just desire, and desire could easily be tamped down.

The thought spurred him, and Jake turned from the window. He climbed the stairs, moved into his temporary office and thrust himself into the chair in front of his computer. The chair that faced the window that looked out onto Tess's house.

Placing his fingers on the keyboard, he looked up at the monitor, ignoring the window beyond, ignoring the slick need that curled through him at the thought of Tess waking up in her bed with only one graveled road between them.

He hit a few keys, deleted what he'd written, then tried again to concentrate his thoughts on his work. Work was all that mattered, all he could count on.

Or almost all he could count on. He could also count on the fact that soon enough, he would be leaving town just as he'd planned. Without even a taste of Tess Buchanan.

And soon enough that damned tree was going to fall on her house—or on her car that appeared to be rusting away—if someone didn't do something about it.

Someone really should do something.

But it wouldn't be him. And it probably didn't matter anyway. His concern wasn't really necessary.

By the time the tree fell, Tess would no doubt be gone from that house. She wouldn't be driving that car. She'd be setting up housekeeping in the biggest mansion in town and parking her shoes beside Grayson Alexander's every night. She'd be warming the man's bed.

And Jake would be back in his own home behind closed doors. He'd probably never see Tess Buchanan again.

Great.

Damn great. That was just the way he wanted things.

Quick and efficient and over in as short a span of time as possible. Jake had been right about the way they should conduct their business, Tess concluded the next day, fighting the knowledge that her eyes were scratchy from lack of sleep, and that Jake had inadvertently been the cause of that sleeplessness…again.

She'd been thinking about him since she'd gotten up an hour ago, a fact that rankled, that embarrassed her. After all, the house was what she was interested in, not the man. Never the man.

He didn't like being here. She didn't like the questions about Jake that persisted in troubling her. How could a man who obviously loved his mother leave her to live out her life alone for long years? How could that same man be persuaded to return solely to save a house that had meant the world to his mother? How could a man who offered to walk a woman home to protect her from the demons of the dark ignore his child's existence?

Tess rubbed at her eyes. She let her breath out in a quick rush. Those questions wouldn't go away, but she didn't want to think about them. She wasn't *going* to think about things she couldn't understand or change. And she'd learned all too well that there were some things she never could change.

So in the end, there was only one thing to be done and that was to do as Jake had asked. She'd do her best to get him out of here as quickly as possible.

That was why, a short time later, Tess was outside his house, camera in hand.

Quietly, she moved about, snapping photos of the west wall, the north wall...the man standing outside the door on the east side of the house.

Tess slowly lowered her camera. It bumped against her breasts as she released her hold, leaving it to dangle from the strap around her neck.

"I—I thought you were probably still sleeping," she said, feeling a sudden need to explain both to herself and to him why she'd been snooping around his property without his knowledge, why she hadn't knocked on his door and explained her presence.

Jake raised his brows. He looked at the sun, which was high in the sky. "Of course," he agreed, although she could read the disbelief in his eyes.

She couldn't help herself, she went ahead and smiled. "I've always been an abominable liar," she admitted. "The truth is that I figured I could just get a bit of work done without...disturbing you at all. I suppose you're wondering why I'm taking pictures of your house."

Shaking his head, Jake stepped forward, descending the stairs to stand beside her. His sudden nearness was disconcerting. Tess just barely managed to stop herself from asking him to move back to his place on the porch.

"I've read some of the materials you gave me, and I assume you're taking some 'before' shots of the house. A historic record of sorts?" Gently Jake reached for her camera, his long fingers brushing against the cotton of her blouse as he grasped the strap and tugged it upward.

"Jake, yes, I—what are you doing?" Tess wrapped her own fingers around the strap, her skin singing where it came in contact with his. "Darn it, taking photos of a house just makes good sense when you're undertaking a restoration project. Maybe I should have asked your permission first, but—"

Slowly, Jake shook his head again. "Take your pictures, Tess," he whispered. "And I don't give a damn whether you ask my permission or not. Take all you want. But first—"

He took advantage of the fact that her grip had slackened with her first words. Whipping the camera away from her, he turned toward her house, dropped to one knee and snapped off a shot.

Startled, Tess stared down at the man kneeling at her feet.

"Jake? What are you doing?"

He aimed the camera higher, took another quick shot, then rose, slipping the strap back over her head. His hands were still looped in the black leather, gently cupping her neck.

"Your tree is ready to topple, lady. I'm just pointing that out to you, taking a 'before' shot of sorts. You'll take care of it?"

Tess felt the trembling start, from the moment his hands touched her hair, her skin. She stepped back quickly, and he released her as she looked up at him.

"It's a sturdy tree." She wondered if her words were more for herself or for him. "It's always been there."

Jake furrowed his brow. "It's a silver maple, Tess. Sturdy enough, but prone to breakage during storms. You still have storms here in Misunderstood, don't you?"

Of course they did. There was a storm taking place right now, deep within her body. A relentless pulsing, a series of shivers made worse by the green fire in his eyes.

Quickly she stepped away, moved toward the side of the house she had yet to capture on film. "I'll research the situation. And...thank you...for caring," she said carefully.

The silence behind her was like thunder waiting to happen.

"Don't thank me. And don't read me wrong, either," he said slowly. "I just figured...hell, it wouldn't look very good if the chairwoman of the Historic Preservation Committee let a tree fall on her house, would it?" he continued, his voice casual, low, and barely there. "No big deal."

Tess wasn't sure what he meant by those last three words, but she was very sure that he meant them, and the hint of sudden unexpected disappointment that slid through her disconcerted. She had been wise to get right to the task, to try to finish with this man as soon as possible.

And that was what she would concentrate on now.

"Now that you've agreed to try to maintain the integrity of the house," she began, "I took the liberty of calling the local historical society the other day. We've managed to unearth two pictures of your house that might be helpful."

Looking over her shoulder, she waited to see if he was following her. "I brought photocopies with me. They're in a folder on the swing. I'm afraid that one of them is a distant shot of the entire area, but the other is relatively clear. Enough detail to be helpful."

When Tess turned from taking the last picture, she found that Jake was barely three feet behind her. The look in his eyes was unsettling. "Why do I have the feeling that you don't get paid for all of this work you do?" he asked.

His accusing tone made her stop. She lifted one shoulder in a shrug, let her lips drift into a hint of a smile. "Maybe because I don't?" she agreed.

When he started to scowl, she forced herself to brave stepping even nearer. "Jake, this is something I just happen to enjoy doing. It's something that matters to me. This town was home to me at a time when I really needed someplace to call my own, and now I enjoy giving back a little. It's...no big deal. Absolutely no big deal," she said, repeating his words.

"Even if I profit from your labor?"

She tilted her head. "I told you that this wouldn't be inexpensive so I doubt you could really say you're profiting in a financial sense, but when it's done—oh Jake— your home is going to be so lovely."

Jake stood still, struck dumb by the sudden light in her violet eyes. Those eyes made a man want to do things he knew damn well he had no business doing. And she'd used those words—"your home"—as if this place really was his home.

What's more, she was going to "research" the situation with the damned tree. He'd just bet she was good at those kinds of things. Heck, he *knew* darn well she *had* to be good at long, slow, detailed research given her position, but this situation called for a little rash behavior, taking quick action and to hell with the research.

"Do you have any other pictures?" she asked suddenly, swallowing hard as he continued to stare at her as though he'd suddenly discovered she was wine and he was thirsty.

Jake held out his hands. "I...really don't have a clue. When my mother went to the nursing home, I hired someone to come in and clean the inside of the house, to box most of her personal effects so that they'd be clean and dry when she came back."

But of course, she hadn't. As far as he knew, all of Flora Walker's things were still in the attic.

"She would have pictures. Plenty of pictures," he reiterated, "but I don't know if there are any of the house."

"Would you...would you like my help? I could look for them with you. There might be some pictures of the interior from years ago."

And she would be in his house again, well within reach of his greedy, grasping hands. Jake hadn't missed that shiver that had slithered through her when his fingers had brushed against her neck. She was being generous to help him, no matter what she said, and he would not betray that generosity. The smart thing to do would be to offer to find his mother's old scrapbooks and photo albums himself.

But Tess was looking up at him like a kid readying herself for a treasure hunt. For the moment she'd forgotten to be skittish. She'd *almost* allowed herself to forget that he'd once done the unforgivable.

His mother would have pictures—and Tess would love to uncover a small bit of town history.

He couldn't deny her.

"Come on," he finally said, holding out one hand. "Let's go search for the Walker family archives."

Sunlight pierced the dusty attic window where Tess knelt a few feet away from Jake, prying open yet another box. They'd gone through ten already and had found only old clothing and bits of bric-a-brac. His mother had surely loved figurines.

But this box was different. Slightly. Underneath a layer of disintegrating tissue were more clothes. Baby clothes. *His* baby clothes most likely. A blue teddy bear with one ear half torn off and missing most of the fur, as if a child had rubbed it off, nearly loved it to death.

Tess found her heart lurching at the thought of Jake as a child, hanging on to that bear for dear life.

The vision was too vivid, too…intimate.

And the child had grown up to become a reckless teenager with a penchant for dangerous situations, Tess knew, remembering Jake's hand on Cassie and the dragon that moved with the muscles beneath his skin.

The teenager had transformed to a man, one with eyes that saw too much, a man who could make her shiver with the merest touch, a man sitting way too close in this suddenly small space. A dangerous man for women as history had proven.

Carefully, Tess placed the bear back inside the box and slowly rose to her feet.

"Perhaps this wasn't such a good idea," she said quietly. "I was too excited to think of it as prying at the time, but now…"

"Now, Tess, it appears that I've hit the jackpot," Jake said in that low, smoky voice of his. He held up a scrapbook, its floral cover faded and worn, the edges rippled and cracked in places.

He held it out and she could no more have withstood the darkening uncertainty of his eyes, the allure he held in his hand, than she could have stopped her blood from sliding through her veins. A family's history was at hand, and for once Jake's smile held no hint of sexual challenge. The curve of his lips was forced and hesitant. Tess was almost sure that he didn't want to open that book, no matter what words he had used to describe his find.

She remembered things she'd heard; that he had been defiant, a challenge to every teacher he'd ever met, from the day he entered school. That wasn't the sign of a happy childhood. This excursion had probably been even more of a mistake than she'd thought just minutes past.

"We don't have to open it," she said simply.

"She kept it." Tess wasn't sure if Jake was talking to her or to himself.

"She kept lots of things."

"Yes. They must have meant something to her, all her things," he said slowly. "What would she have thought, knowing I'd left them to rot here?"

"The woman I met was proud of her son. She mentioned you once. She would have merely thought...that you had your own life."

"And she had hers, one that centered around this house, these boxes," he admitted. "Come have a look, Tess. She liked you, you said. My guess, then, is that she would have wanted to share these with you."

It was an invitation she couldn't refuse, because it was the truth, and because no matter what he'd done, she knew that he needed someone beside him when he faced the past for the first time in years.

Sliding closer, very near, Tess dropped to her knees.

She reached out to the book he still held and pulled back the heavy cover.

The first pages were old, the photos black and white. A birthday party in progress on the lawn in front of the house at a time when all the decorative woodwork was still in place. Crowds of children stood like little soldiers with carefully posed smiles and cake smeared on their faces.

A low chuckle escaped Jake's lips, and Tess knew what he was thinking. No ghosts of his past here. Nothing to avoid, no memories of darker days. Just hope and fun and a darn good picture of the house, better than the one she'd brought.

Tess turned to him then, a small, satisfied smile lifting her lips—and found her mouth only inches from his own.

She breathed in, suddenly, deeply, and her senses were filled with the scent of smoky after-shave, soap and…warm male. He was close, so close, her breath mingled with his.

If she wanted to, she could move into his arms just by leaning slightly. She could run her hand along that rigid, square jawline by merely sliding her hand forward a touch. The flesh of her palm would drag against the dark shadows where his beard was already roughening his skin. In half a breath, her fingertips could slip against the midnight silk of his hair.

If *he* really wanted to, he could cover her mouth with his own. Easily.

In the still of the moment she looked up into his eyes. Jake's fingers swept a path across her cheek. He curled his palm around the nape of her neck, gently urging her closer.

Tess swayed slightly, brushing up against the soft cotton of his shirt.

She was going to be kissed by Jake Walker. She was going to touch him. His lips against hers. Now.

The thought formed, sizzled its way through her brain, blazing a path of clarity and reason. Tess stiffened, sucked in a great gulp of air.

Jake swore softly beneath his breath, releasing his gentle hold on her.

Lurching upward, her mind a silent swirl of guilt and confusion, Tess clenched and unclenched those hands that had nearly betrayed her. She stared straight into deep green eyes that had turned suddenly fierce and angry.

"It's never smart to get too close to a dragon, Tess." Jake's voice was husky and dry. He rose, leaning forward to avoid hitting his head on the low, sloping ceiling, and Tess stepped back, farther away. Her sandal slid on the piece of tissue she'd taken from the box and Jake reached out automatically to catch her, then quickly brought his hands back to his sides.

Regaining her balance, she looked up at him.

"I should finish taking some pictures of the interior of the house...so that you'll have a complete record once you begin demolition." She bit her lip, knowing her words, her tone, were stilted. An idiot could see right through the excuse to the discomfort that lay beneath, and Jake was no idiot.

"That seems like a real good idea," he agreed, shoving his hands into his back pockets. "I'll bring the albums downstairs. Maybe you'd like to take them home to see if there's anything of value in them."

The automatic urge to protest, to tell him that they were *his* family's photos, rose up inside her, but she tamped it back down. He didn't want to look at those pictures. *She* didn't want to put herself in the position of sitting that near to him again.

It was unavoidably clear that she was still harboring some of those silly girlhood fantasies she'd once been prone to, that a part of her was still susceptible to Jake's dark sensuality, still wanting to believe that she was the mouse capable of taming the lion when no one else could.

But the fact was that he *was* an untrustworthy lion, and she was not the person who could change him. She had no right to even think along those lines. She was marrying Gray. She cared for Gray. And she was way too old to be chasing cotton-candy daydreams.

Right now what she needed was a good strong dose of illusion-shattering reality. Caffeine for the soul.

Tess took a deep calming breath. She stared Jake dead in the eye.

"When I'm done, I'll take the albums home," she agreed, her voice quiet and as calm as she could make it. "And I'll let you know if I find anything interesting. They're probably mostly pictures of you. Parents always seem to want lots of photos of their children."

The comment sailed into the silence like a rock shattering glass. Shocking, as she'd meant it to be. Like smelling salts or a punch to the gut, her words were meant to focus all thought on the bottom line, the truth that she had to keep forcing herself to remember. He was an absentee father. She'd wager a year's worth of paychecks that he had no pictures of his son.

And she didn't have to wonder whether Jake understood her meaning. She could see that he did.

His face became a mask. Casual, empty of emotion. He nodded in her direction. "You told me you were stubborn. I see that you were right."

Tess could have dropped it there. She didn't want to.

"When was the last time you saw Cassie?" she asked, wishing her voice had come out stronger, less sad.

Jake studied the slender woman in front him. Her eyes were wary and yet filled with sorrow; tired, as if the task of dealing with him was just too much. He'd been told many times that it was, and he knew what she was trying to do.

They'd been too close back there, he'd nearly snaked his arm around her waist and done what he'd been wanting to do. He'd damn near wrapped himself around her, touched her in a way she would have regretted.

Clearly, she realized that as well as he did, and she needed some space. She needed to remind herself that he was a darker shade of dangerous than she was used to dealing with. And the deeply responsible woman who lived within her wanted him to come clean, to face what she saw as his responsibilities.

He'd never expected to react again when someone assumed the worst of him. He had no right to be bothered now. After all, he was the one perpetuating the lie. But it was a lie that *had* to be perpetuated. He wouldn't let a child suffer so that he could win a woman's smile for even a second. And besides, it was probably best that this woman thought him guilty as sin. After all, he never would be tame enough for someone like her and he wouldn't want to be, no matter what. But the small, certain ache was there. It caught him sure and strong, dead center of the chest.

"I don't remember when I last saw her," he confessed. It was the truth. He didn't remember the date. Sometime a few months ago. He'd tried to offer Cassie help, but she'd taken his hand and refused. She only needed his friendship, she insisted. And she'd sent back the money he'd slipped into her purse when she wasn't looking. "I...really can't remember."

There was a war going on within Tess's eyes. She had wanted to think that he was a responsible father. She had not been totally immune to him as a man, and she didn't like that. No, not at all.

He didn't like it, either. He didn't like the way he had to keep reminding himself that she wore an invisible Do Not Touch sign. He didn't like the fact that he even wanted to get close enough to get caught up in the honeysuckle scent of her. And no way did he like the fact that he wanted a woman who was a part of Gray Alexander's world. He didn't want to get to know anyone in this town, especially not Tess.

And so he would help her maintain that distance between them.

"I'll pack the boxes. You go take the rest of your pictures. We might accomplish more if we divide the tasks and work on our own as much as possible."

And he might just go totally crazy before this whole episode was through.

There was only one thing that was certain. He was going to have to educate himself quickly, to learn what needed to be done, and to do as much as possible without Tess's help.

He was going to have to dive into this project headfirst if he wanted out fast.

And there was nothing Jake was more sure of than that. He was going to do everything in his power to finish up here and put lots of snarled and twisting roads between himself and Tess Buchanan.

If the roads stretched on far enough, if there were enough miles between them, maybe then, just maybe, he could manage to keep his hands off of her.

Chapter Five

Tess was off early the next day, but not so early that Jake didn't notice her departure. He'd noticed a few other things, too. She'd been on foot when she left, but the sky had slipped from blue to gray now. The wind was beginning to whistle. He wondered if her car had finally refused to start or if she'd simply needed to walk off a few things. He wondered if she was still regretting the fact that he'd nearly given in to temptation and molded his body to her own yesterday.

Not that it mattered. No, not at all. He was still going to have to go after her. There was still a chance that she could get caught in the storm, and there was no way he could ignore that fact.

The damn woman was probably out doing more research on his house, or developing those pictures she'd taken yesterday. Film and photos he should be paying for. That alone was enough to send him out into the gathering clouds.

Tess Buchanan might as well learn one thing right

now. He might bow to her authority in the end, he might have to shove his plans beneath her nose and those of her committee members to get anything done, but now that she had supplied him with the information he needed, he was damn well capable of doing his own research, making his own plans, taking as many photographs or measurements as necessary. He should never have allowed her to get involved in this or to come into his house or his life, and he was darn well going to make sure she knew he didn't really need her anymore.

He would pay for those photos and anything else she'd done or know the reason why. There was no way he was going to have Tess living with regrets where he was concerned—or paying for things he should be doing himself.

It was still early, and the town was barely waking up when Tess slipped into town. Only the gas station, the diner, and Bickerson's Drugs had opened their doors. Only one or two lumbering autos were creeping along the tree-shaded streets, so the rumble from the motorcycle growing louder as it neared was like a siren's song, a beacon of sound that drew the attention of the few people who had ventured out onto the streets.

Tess turned, her hand resting on the slick handle of the door leading into the drugstore. She had a ridiculous urge to flatten herself against the side of the building. Jake was probably on his way to the grocery store just on the other side of town. She didn't want him to see her or to feel that he had to acknowledge her in some way.

She wasn't sure she wanted to talk to him. Not yet, anyway. Not when she was still shaking from the totally unacceptable and absolutely...naive feelings that had coursed through her yesterday.

She wasn't a kid anymore. Neither was Jake. She could no longer absolve him of guilt where Cassie was concerned.

And willingly or not, he was messing with her happiness, tempting her in ways she didn't want to be tempted. So it was better to act the fool and coward now than to take such a risk.

Tess took a deep breath. She watched as Jake banked the corner just a block away and headed in her direction. The wind whipped his shirt against his chest, and she noted the way his strong thighs gripped the cycle's saddle. He was power, masculinity personified.

He was only a few stores away right now.

Turning, Tess pushed on the door, hard. It opened slightly. The jingling of the bell announced her entrance.

Behind her, the cycle's engine halted, fading away to silence.

Resisting the urge to look over her shoulder, she hastened into the air-conditioned store.

But when the bell rattled behind her once again, she couldn't stop herself from sucking in a deep, nervous breath. She couldn't play the game anymore.

Turning, Tess looked into Jake's eyes. She felt the heated flush climbing up beneath her blouse as he watched her. He knew darn well that she'd heard him coming and that she'd tried to avoid him. He remembered perfectly *why* she'd wanted to maintain some distance.

But, "Tess, it's going to rain," was all he said.

"I know, but home is just a few blocks from here, and I'm not staying long, anyway," she managed. "I just had a minor errand to tend to."

He held out his hand, palm up.

"Fine. I'll take care of the developing, and the film I should have paid for yesterday."

Tess shook her head. She crossed her arms, not even bothering to dig around in her purse for what he wanted.

"How do you know my being here has anything to do with developing pictures of your house? I could be here for any number of reasons." She tilted her head, studying him. She knew Craig Bickerson was watching them from behind the register. Jake had to know it, too, but he wasn't acknowledging the man. His gaze was fastened on her. Unwavering. Unsmiling.

"Like what?"

Immediately Tess raised her head. She looked around, her gaze falling on the displays of diapers, of magnifying reading glasses, a bold and eye-catching wall of condoms.

"Aspirin," she whispered quickly, swallowing in spite of herself.

She glared at Jake.

He was smiling just as if he'd known what she'd been looking at, what she'd been thinking.

"Maybe aspirin," he agreed. "But I'd bet my next advance check that you've also got an undeveloped roll of film in that purse. Because you promised me speed and efficiency, and because you're not the type to waste time. Yesterday you took photos. It stands to reason you'd be taking care of the next order of business today. You wouldn't leave that roll of film lying around gathering dust. You're much too responsible."

The way he said it sounded almost like an insult. "Anything wrong with that?" she asked.

Jake's smile was grim. "Absolutely nothing. Now let

me have the film, Tess. While we're standing here talking, the rain is coming.''

She didn't budge. It was silly to protest so much over nothing, but the truth was that she had always been a little bit out of control every time in her life she'd been near Jake. She needed to be in control now. She didn't want him slipping her money every time she made some minor investment in this project. It was too personal, way too unsettling.

"Jake, this is something I chose to do," she said.

"It's my house and you're not even paid for all your trouble," he reminded her unnecessarily. He moved a touch closer, reaching into his back pocket. Pulling out his wallet, he extracted a bill and began to tuck it into the side of her purse.

Instinctively she backed away.

"Tess," he growled.

"No," she insisted, a little too loudly.

"Is there a problem here?" Craig's voice sliced into the conversation like a knife that came from nowhere. His words echoed through the almost-empty store, too near the same words that had been uttered to her years ago on that day she and Jake had come together before. Tess wondered if Jake was remembering, too, or if he'd even heard anything that had been said that day.

Jake stared into Tess's worried eyes, then glanced up at the man barreling his way down the aisle toward the two of them. *Is there a problem here, Walker?* He'd heard those words a thousand times before, and hell, half the time he'd merited them.

He'd been able to drive Craig's father crazy just by stepping into the store. Bailey Bickerson had followed his every move, openly trailed him, as if *he* had been the Walker who had robbed a man at gunpoint two counties over.

Craig himself had always looked at Jake as if he expected to have his milk money taken by force. Jake could make him fidget with just one dark glance. But years had gone by. Bailey had retired to Arizona five years ago. Craig owned this store now, and he no longer resembled a shivering puppy cowering before the bogeyman.

He looked a whole heck of a lot like his father had, and right now he also looked like a justifiably righteous man defending his territory—or his favorite lady.

Jake swallowed that bit of insight and found himself admiring Craig just a touch even as the dark claw of resentment rose up within him. He was glad to know that someone at least was looking out for Tess's interests. She certainly had no real sense of self-preservation as far as he could see. He wondered just how brave Craig had become, and how far he would go in his defense of the lady in question, if it would be far enough.

Raising one brow in a practiced threatening move that Craig was sure to recognize, Jake crossed his arms. He stared back at the broad-chested boxerlike man who met his gaze head-on.

"Can I help you in some way, Tess?" Craig said, almost gently for such a great ox of a man. He turned to her as if Jake wasn't even standing there.

Tess stared at Jake, her face turning a delicious pink as Craig waited for her response. "I—no, I'm fine, Craig," she finally said, throwing one hand out in a gesture of frustration.

"You don't look as if everything is fine," the man protested, beetling his eyebrows.

His thoughts exactly, Jake admitted. Tess looked flustered, cornered. Her eyes had that wary expression he'd seen in his own mirror this morning. And it was his fault, it seemed. He was bringing trouble into a good woman's life again, and damn it, he didn't want to do that. No way. If the truth were told, ever since he'd seen her gazing at those old pictures and speaking of his mother with such respect and admiration, he'd been toying with the idea of giving in and turning his house into the kind of beauty he knew she'd be proud of. He wanted to help her add another notch to her belt. Like it or not, he found himself wanting to make things as easy for her as he could.

But he still wasn't going to let her pay his way.

"We'll talk more about this later," he said, turning to leave. No point in embarrassing the lady further in front of her friend. He'd wait outside, then take her home out of the wet.

"We'll talk about it now." Tess's voice dropped into the silent store bell-clear.

Jake raised one brow. She was taking that totally-in-charge schoolteacher stance. She sounded tough, in control, and he had no doubt that she could handle a classroomful of charging students—or Craig Bickerson. But he wasn't fooled. He'd seen her eyes go soft and troubled. He knew she had some very vulnerable spots. She wasn't made of steel, like him. And he was pretty darn certain that she didn't like scenes.

So the fact that she was standing her ground when he'd given her an out caught him square in the gut.

She turned to Craig. "Thank you for your concern, Craig, but there is absolutely nothing wrong. Mr. Walker is a gentleman and he was not assaulting me, robbing me, or in any other way, shape or form, bothering me. We were simply having a business disagreement."

Damn it, the woman was actually defending him, trying to make him look like a prince to a man who'd more than once seen him at his worst and knew that terming him a "gentleman" was a total lie.

He didn't need or want anyone defending him.

Jake glared at her, put his hand up to stop her. But he needn't have worried. Craig didn't look at all convinced.

Tess opened her mouth again.

"Don't say any more, Tess," Jake growled. "Just take care of your business and we'll settle this outside before I take you home. I don't want you getting caught in the storm."

He felt rather than saw Craig's appraising glance turn toward him, but it was Tess, not the druggist's son, who held his attention right now.

Jake held out one hand as if to draw her closer to the door, but he didn't touch her.

She eyed the hand that still held the bill suspiciously, then looked to where Craig stood watching their every move. Slowly she nodded.

"Let me just fill out the form for the development. It's silly to make such a big deal out of my taking a few pictures. As a teacher, I buy little things for my classroom all the time, just like every other teacher in America. But if it really bothers you, I'll agree to keep a record of the few expenses I incur and you can repay me before you leave town."

Turning toward Craig, Tess tilted her head. "I think you get the drift, Craig. Mr. Walker and I have resolved our problems." And pushing past both men, she made her way to the other end of the store.

Like hell, they'd resolved their problems, Jake thought, admiring the soft swing of her hair and the slender curve of her back as she wandered the aisles. He was still burning with thirst for a small taste of her lips when he couldn't even consider drinking.

There were mountains and fences between them, barriers that could never be breached. The truth of what he was and what she was and would be, the lies that couldn't be set straight. She did things to him that he didn't even want to think about, called forth longings he couldn't afford to examine.

No, he and Tess Buchanan would never resolve their problems. He ought to feel glad about that, because if there were no locked gates between them, Jake wasn't sure he could trust himself around her. Heck, that was a lie. He knew darn well that if there was nothing keeping them apart, there'd be no stopping him. He'd be doing his damnedest to woo her into his bed.

And that kind of action could only hurt a lady like her.

So he should be doubly glad that she still thought him a villain in at least one way, because if she ever turned the full light of those beautiful eyes of hers on him, if she ever looked at him with total trust, he'd take her down with him. No question. Her name would be on every gossip's tongue in no time.

It was an incredibly good thing that she didn't completely trust him. Jake repeated that thought over and over to himself as he left Craig standing alone and in silence and made his own way outside to wait for his beautiful and bravely stubborn neighbor.

Tess stared at the Harley as if it had teeth. When she had agreed to what Jake was asking, she hadn't thought this far ahead, but now here he was, holding a helmet out to her, obviously expecting her to climb aboard.

Glancing up and away from him, she looked at the threatening sky. The wind was whipping wildly now.

"Forget it. There's no way you're walking home," he said. "Not in this kind of weather. If we hurry, we can just beat the thing." He reached out and brushed his hand against her cheek, pushing her hair back off her face. Gently he lowered the helmet onto her head.

She let him.

"Were you expecting company?" she asked, indicating the helmet that afforded her a bit of protection from that shattering green gaze of his.

"No, not at all." He climbed onto the Harley and motioned for her to seat herself behind him. "And all I'm expecting now is for you to get your sweet little rear end on board and hang on tight, so we can get the hell out of here. A cycle may get us home faster than walking, but it's not the vehicle of choice when the roads are slick."

It was that, the knowledge that he had waited for her and she was keeping him, possibly placing him and herself in danger by hesitating, that convinced Tess to throw one leg over the wide seat and wrap her arms around Jake's waist. She'd barely settled when they were off and flying.

And then there was no possibility of talking. The air rushed by like a cyclone. The only possibility for cover, Jake's broad back.

That was the only reason she was clinging to him, Tess told herself. She was a neophyte on a motorcycle, and he would be used to the feel of a woman riding behind him. He wouldn't think twice about the clasp of her hands against his stomach, probably wouldn't even notice the warmth where her body touched his back. It certainly wouldn't make his heart start revving like the cycle's engine. He wouldn't be nervous or confused.

And neither should she, Tess thought as the drops began to splash about her, pinging off the helmet's surface. The house was only a few doors down now, and the ride was over, anyway.

There was no time to worry about her own troublesome sensations—or even the lightning and rain. As Jake came to a stop in front of her house, she shot off the back to make it easier for him to effect his own escape. Immediately he took her hand and pulled her toward her stairs, up under the slope of her porch roof.

Fat drops hit the stairs, faster now, falling thick and noisily. Jake took his helmet off. He accepted the one she was holding out to him.

"Be seeing you, Tess." His voice was the only calm thing in this tangled swirl of wind and water and rumbling thunder. He stepped out, angling toward the edge of the porch, clearly intending to go. She wondered if his only reason for having gone into town was to save her from getting caught out in the weather, but of course, that was nonsense. He'd probably simply been distracted from his original purpose.

And now? His house was only across the street, but the storm was still holding. There was no way he could make it even a few feet without getting totally drenched.

"Wait," she urged, barely resting her fingertips on his forearm. "I'm sure it won't take long for the rain to stop."

A muscle tensed in his arm, but he stopped where he stood. He turned to look at her as she reclaimed her hand.

One dark eyebrow rose, and his mouth tipped up in a

grin. "You seem to spend a lot of time reassuring me that things won't take long, Tess."

"You're so eager to be gone, then? From this town, I mean?"

He stared at her, studied her, nearly looked right into her mind, it almost seemed.

She took a deep breath and refused to look away.

"I need to be gone," he agreed. "By the way, I meant to tell you that I've read most of the materials you've given me, and located a bit more information here and there," he said slowly, easing even closer to the lip of the porch. "I'm pretty sure I can do a lot of this work on my own. That will leave you free to those students you tutor. It will give you more time to spend with Gray. You have to have been giving up a fair share of your leisure hours lately."

Tess knew better than to examine the reasons why her breath caught in her throat just then.

"You'll need measurements, detailed drawings. You'll need to either hire an architect or general contractor, someone who's familiar with old houses and knows something about preservation."

"And then I'll need to get the town and the preservation committee's blessing before the actual work can begin," he finished for her. "I know all that, Tess. The information you supplied me with was very thorough."

The wind caught in the butterfly wind chime overhead, causing it to shiver and ring in an unsteady rhythm like the breath that was soughing in and out of Tess's body. He was trying to help her, trying to free her from this unwelcome entanglement. She should be grateful, she *would* be grateful when she had time to think things through. Tess was sure of it.

She stared into his eyes. He was waiting for her to

agree with him. The wind chime jingled, demanding a response.

He shook his head, looked at the mix of ceramic monarchs, swallowtails and painted ladies.

"Butterflies," he said simply. "You seem to have a taste for them." He glanced down at the golden chain at her neck. She hoped that he couldn't see that her pulse had quickened with his perusal.

She nodded curtly. "I like the real ones better. They seem to prefer your yard. You have the right plants."

He tilted his head, questioning her.

"My passion may be butterflies, but my specialty is *houses*," she emphasized. "No green thumb." She held her hands out for inspection. The wind was fading slightly, the rain was beginning to slacken just a touch. He would be gone in a minute. She would be glad.

"You're sure you don't need my help?" she asked suddenly, her voice stiff and stilted. He would think she was merely being polite. She wondered if she was.

"I understand most of what needs to be done, and I'm used to working alone," he assured her. "But if you're worried about the house, I promise to contact you if I run into any snags. I'll definitely consult with you before I attempt to approach the committee for approval."

A small sense of relief flooded Tess's soul. She wasn't sure why, but she knew that she didn't want Jake facing the committee alone.

"Craig's not on the committee," she said softly.

A smile lifted Jake's lips. "I assume you're trying to reassure me," he said. "So, who besides you is on the infamous committee? Anyone I would know?"

She stared at him. "One or two." The words barely slipped through her teeth.

Jake waited.

"Mrs. Jackson is the secretary." A nice, motherly woman who had moved in only five years ago and wouldn't hold a grudge against anyone, anyway. "And Reverend Harper has been a member for two years." Also a newcomer, and immensely fair and open-minded. "There's also—"

She hesitated.

Jake reached out and touched his fingertip to her frozen lips. "Also?"

Looking up into his eyes, Tess stared straight ahead. "There's also Dora Averly." A former teacher who had always sworn that Jake led her straight into early retirement. "And...Grayson."

Jake's hand stilled at that. He raised both brows, nodded his head in acceptance.

"Whatever happened between you and Gray?" she asked suddenly.

He stared at her, his expression calm, still. "What did you hear?" he asked.

"That it was in the past and nothing important," she repeated.

Jake shrugged. "Then I guess it was, and I guess you should really be asking Gray," he said.

"But I'm asking you, Jake. It might be important when the time comes."

He shook his head. "You don't want to know."

"I'm not a child."

Jake jerked his head up, locked his gaze on hers. "I never said you were."

"But you're trying to protect me now, just the way Gray is. I know that was what he was doing."

"Tess." The word was a groan. Jake rested his hands on his hips, looked to the side. "Oh, what the hell. You want to know what was between me and Gray? All right, then. That's easy. That's simple. He brought a girl to the dance, I took her home. He blackened my eye, I broke his nose. It was a long time ago. I was fifteen to his sixteen. Past history. Long gone.''

"And why did you do that? Why did you walk away with Gray's date?''

He stared at her long and hard. There was nothing soft about the look in his eyes, the taut line of his lips.

"I walked away with Gray's girl...because I could,'' he explained. "Just because I could.''

There was still a fine mist falling as Jake moved away from her house and climbed on his cycle. He rode away down the street, the dampness settling about him. He would be wet through and through in no time.

But Tess didn't call him back. She didn't have the voice to do so. She didn't have the presence of mind to even collect her thoughts properly.

All she knew was that Jake had stolen Grayson's date simply because the girl had wanted him more than she'd wanted Gray.

He was warning her that he was a man who didn't care, but then she already knew that was true.

And that it wasn't, at least not completely.

He cared about some things. He cared enough to warn her to watch her step around him.

She should be grateful at least for that. It was a good thing that Jake had decided to keep his distance. Surely it was a very good thing.

Chapter Six

Only an idiot or a heartless devil would have said those words to Tess. Jake lay in the dark, one bare arm propped behind his head as he stared at the cracks in the milky plaster overhead.

He'd known that she was skittish around him, that it was only her admirable sense of duty and the sheer courage of the lady that kept her there working with him, and yet he'd said the one thing that was destined to spook her and make her run. He'd deliberately aimed the dart straight at her sense of fair play and justice.

It had hit home, he was sure that it had.

No matter that he couldn't even remember the name of the girl he and Gray had once butted horns over, no matter that Gray probably couldn't, either. They'd both been young studs, full of pride and anger and testosterone and the girl had dumped them both for the captain of the football team the very next week. No matter. He'd once envied the easy manners and smooth ways born in

Alexander. Gray had always bristled at his own tendency to cross the line when he felt it needed to be crossed.

He'd crossed the line with Tess, he'd nearly kissed her the other day, and he was tempted by her daily.

But no way would he give in to that temptation. He would stay out of her hair, out of her way, and he would do his damnedest to get the wheels rolling so that when he left, this house would be a home that would have pleased his mother and would fill Tess with pride, knowing that it was her influence that had brought it back to life.

For the first time in a long time, he wanted to be a better man than he had been. He wanted to bring a smile to a lady's lips.

A shaft of something sharp and uncomfortable and horribly rusty slid through Jake, lodging in his chest.

Longing, the need for soul-to-soul trust rose up in him.

He dismissed it. Deliberately. Ruthlessly.

He had lied to her, and he didn't regret the lie. He had pushed away her offer of help and he couldn't allow himself to regret that. It was best for all concerned.

But for one sweet moment he wished he could meet Tess on common ground, no lies between them, no barriers of personality or background or circumstance. For one hour of time, he wanted to touch her, without and within, to share her smiles and the bliss of her body. He wanted the power to make her glow with happiness and not regret the glowing afterward.

That wasn't a possibility, not at all. And he'd never let it happen even if it were.

She had the man meant to bring her that happiness.

Jake met the truth head on. He would leave Tess alone.

But he could still wish and want.

A man could always do that, no matter what.

Tess tutored her students. She cleaned her house even though it didn't need cleaning. She went out to dinner with Grayson, smiling when he told her stories about what was happening in town while she was home teaching algebra and English.

"I hear that you and Jake have parted ways," he said casually over coffee.

Tess raised one brow. "And you're wondering why I didn't mention that small fact, aren't you?"

Gray's smile was genuine. "Have I told you how much I've always admired your honest and direct approach?"

Shrugging, Tess smiled. "I was going to tell you, of course. Jake's got things under control for now. He's taking measurements, reviewing all the recommendations that have been made and going over the house inch by inch. He doesn't need my help right now."

"But he may in time." It was a grim statement, his gaze direct and questioning.

Tess smoothed her napkin out, pleating the edge with precision. "I'm not leaving the dance with him, Gray."

Silence slid in.

"Told you that, did he?"

"Let's just say that I demanded information. I'm in charge of seeing that this project doesn't encounter any roadblocks, and much as I care for you, I know that he isn't your favorite person."

Gray studied her carefully. "You think I'd be unfair because of some prior tiff I'd had with a guy?"

Tess blinked, blew out her breath. "No, I guess you wouldn't. All right, I know that you wouldn't, Grayson.

You wear the white hat, but…he's still an irritation to you.''

Shaking his head, Grayson smiled. "I'm not holding a grudge, Tess. Heck, I'm not sure I wouldn't have done the same thing if the tables had been turned in those days. Jake and I had been adversaries ever since my father testified against his father in court. But the truth is that Jake can't be trusted. I was there the day he spilled twenty dollars' worth of merchandise out of his pockets in front of Bailey Bickerson's cash register just to prove to the man that he could steal if he really wanted to. I heard Bailey order him never to come back in his store. I haven't forgotten that Jake offered up that insolent smile of his when Bailey threatened to hit him…and I haven't forgiven him for what he did to Cassandra Pratt. He got her expelled, Tess."

Sucking in her breath, Tess clenched her napkin tightly. "*I* did that. You know that. And he tried to plead her case."

Gray shook his head. "Too easy to do that afterward. She wouldn't have been expelled at all if he hadn't been so eager to have her."

Grayson's voice was harsh and unforgiving, a slick, sharp blade, ripping away at all her arguments. She didn't know all that had happened between Cassie and Jake that day, she couldn't condemn him for that…but she knew what had happened afterward. Jake had deserted a baby.

"I'll do my job, Gray, when the time comes. Until then, please stop worrying. I'm not a vulnerable high school student."

He held out his hands. "All right, you're a super-smart, highly efficient, indisputably independent woman, which is exactly what I admire about you. I'll do my best to stop trying to interfere in your business.''

Lifting her hand in his own, he kissed her fingertips. The press of his lips on her skin should have warmed her and made her long for more, but that didn't happen. True, her relationship with him had never been based on passion. They were the best of friends. But their brief touches had always been pleasurable, she was sure their marriage would be fulfilling. And yet today she hadn't felt even a hint of desire, just friendship, and maybe that *was* a problem she could lay at Jake's door. The man had caught her attention. He had completely distracted her, and the last thing she wanted was to be distracted by a man who played at being honorable only when it pleased him.

But she couldn't help noticing how he carefully cleaned away the debris in his mother's yard; she couldn't help remembering the regret in his voice when he spoke of Flora.

She couldn't help thinking that he had deliberately forced her away.

And that there was more here than met the eye. She'd lived in small towns long enough to know that there were always stories buried beneath stories.

And so it was that Tess found herself at midnight poring over the pages of Flora Walker's scrapbooks.

She looked at Jake's baby pictures, the small but happy family. She read the accounts of Frank Walker's arrest on armed-robbery charges, of his death while driving drunk a few weeks after he was finally set free.

But mostly she noticed how Jake stopped smiling in his photos for a long time after his father's disappearance from the scene. She noticed that the children in his childhood pictures changed from those sons and daughters of the cream of Misunderstood's upper echelon to the sons and daughters of the down and out. And often Jake was alone. Far too often Jake's smile was defiant. And way, way too often, the pages in that scrapbook were spotted with long-dried tears. Flora Walker's tears, Tess assumed.

Tess couldn't help wondering about the woman and about her relationship with her son. She wondered most of all what kinds of things Flora Walker cried about at night. She wondered why Jake had left a woman who had loved her son so much she'd chronicled his life in detail long after many parents had stopped taking pictures beyond birthdays and Christmas. Flora had saved every Mother's Day card Jake had given her, every report card. These books were a testament to her love for her son. And yet Jake had gone away and left her.

There were letters, many letters he had written her, letters Tess wouldn't read. They weren't, after all, meant for her eyes. Still, the man had gone. Flora had lived her last years without him.

He had left this town alone.

And he was still alone in a town where he had lived eighteen years of his life. He courted solitude, had purposely tried to drive her away.

And she had let him. Even though she was the expert. She knew more about that house than he possibly could, for all his experience as a researcher. And she knew the people he would need to know. She'd worked with them.

Still, she'd let Jake talk her off this project. Or rather, she'd run from this project and this man. She'd turned coward the way she had once long ago...because Jake reminded her that she hadn't always been smart about men, because he touched her in ways she couldn't afford to be touched, and mostly because she was susceptible to him.

"So deal with it, Buchanan," she ordered herself, rising up out of her chair. "Now that you've admitted it, deal with it."

She was strong, she had learned her lessons, and she was proud of this town and her accomplishments with it. She would not walk away from her responsibilities just because Jake made her nervous, made her want in impossible, unacceptable ways. There was work here and she was in charge of it. She was no frail, crushable flower, and she would take care of things no matter what.

So, picking up the scrapbook, Tess stepped out into the sunlight. She marched across the street. Guided by the faint sounds that hinted of human habitation, she made her way around Jake's yard to the grassy area behind the house where he was scraping paint from the clapboards low on the building.

For long seconds she just stood watching, silent, as his scraper thunked against the punky texture of the weathered wood.

"The sill needs replacing, but it's doable," she said quietly, wanting to snag his attention, but not sure what to say.

He glanced up, no trace of surprise in his eyes. A half smile lifted his lips and he shook his head, rising from his crouched position near the ground, the muscles in his thighs flexing beneath his faded denims.

"So the committee sent you here for a progress report?" he asked.

Tess hugged the scrapbook tighter. She looked him square in the face.

"Not the committee. Just me this time. I brought your scrapbook back with some notes." She held it out for him to see, then shook her head impatiently. "But that's not the real reason I'm here. I...shouldn't have allowed you to send me away in the first place. You can use my assistance."

Jake rested his hand on the sunlit, scarred wood of the old house. "You have a sense of duty that lies deep in your soul, Tess. Don't you ever throw responsibility to the wind?"

Not lately. Not since following her emotions had caused her such grief in the past.

"Duty's not such a bad thing," she said quietly.

He stared at her, hard. She knew he thought she was reprimanding him and that hadn't been her intent at all. She didn't approve of things he'd done, but she knew very well that this man ran deeper than people thought. He was not hers to judge.

Slowly she smiled. "My sense of duty is going to save you some trouble. What stage of the game are you at?"

He released a breath and gave her a wicked grin. "The stage I'm going to hate. Interviewing general contractors."

Tess allowed her smile to blossom. "It just so happens that I personally know every general contractor in the area. I can introduce you. I know what questions to ask which people. Are you going to walk away from my expertise when it can speed up the process for you?"

Jake lay his paint scraper on the porch. He pushed one hand back through that thick, black mane of his as if he wasn't exactly thrilled with the situation and didn't like having his choices spelled out in such black-and-white terms. Then he held out both hands in a gesture of surrender.

"You're a fool to be here, Tess. Even I don't trust myself half the time."

There was no question that he was talking about their near embrace the week before.

She hesitated, bit at her dry lips. "That was...an unusual circumstance," she offered, not sure whether she was trying to convince herself or him.

"Damn right it was unusual. I don't let myself get caught off guard or carried away by the moment."

His gaze was direct, laser-sharp and hot.

Tess swallowed hard. "Then we'll be fine."

He opened his mouth to speak, then clamped it shut again, digging his hands deep into his pockets. "I've got the list you gave me. Who do you want to call first?"

Breathing a sigh of relief, Tess relaxed slightly. "No one. We're going to be a bit unorthodox about this. I've found that you can discover a lot about the way a man works by cornering him in his lair, so to speak. Today we're going to do some drop-ins on contractors in the area, visit the offices of those who have them in the county, some sites where others are working. You'll learn a lot, I guarantee you."

A low chuckle escaped Jake. "Oh, Tess, that let's-get-down-to-business look in your eyes when you talk that teacher talk does strange things to me."

"It probably reminds you of all those times you spent warming the chair in the principal's office," she said jokingly, then instantly regretted her insensitive comment. She opened her eyes wide, slipped her palm up over her lips. "That was..."

"Impulsive, Tess," Jake said with a smile. "And probably correct to some extent, but I can absolutely guarantee you that Principal Rivers never had me admiring the way the sun glinted off his hair the way you do."

Tess couldn't hold back her own answering grin. "I

guess he wouldn't.'' J.D. Rivers had always had a short-age of hair and was rather proud of the stern look it gave him.

"All right, I'm ready for an education," Jake con-ceded. "And, Tess, thank you. You're a brave woman."

"Maybe," she agreed, "but not brave enough to chance that cycle of yours again. Would you mind if I drove my car?"

Jake took the scrapbook she was holding out to him. "Not at all. I've been wanting to get a closer look at your car, anyway. You need a good mechanic."

She nodded, turning toward her house. "I'll do some research on the matter."

Tess was almost sure she could hear Jake swearing behind her, but she didn't turn. She was all too aware of his eyes at her back, suddenly too cognizant of herself as a woman.

Thank goodness she wasn't going to be clinging to him on the back of a motorcycle today. At least she wouldn't have those kinds of distractions.

But Tess hadn't counted on the distraction of having Jake beside her with only the paltry width of a gearshift separating their bodies. She hadn't figured on what it would be like to be closed up in the small space of a car with him—or on the fact that every time she glanced down or to the side, her gaze came smack up against...Jake. The man was larger than life, much too disconcerting. With his seat pushed back as far as it would go to accommodate the long length of his legs, he was slightly behind her. She could feel her skin prick-ling each time he glanced her way. It was as if he sur-rounded her, as if he caressed her—or was thinking about caressing her.

"The first stop's not far away," she rasped, moving into a turn a bit too fast.

Silence followed her comment. Then she felt Jake's hand barely touching her own, clenched too tightly on the wheel.

"Relax, Tess. I'm hardly likely to attempt a seduction at forty miles an hour. You're safe. But then, I intended that you would be that, anyway. Even standing still."

Alarmed at how easily the man could get to her, ashamed for being such a baby, Tess took a deep breath.

"Don't mind me. I'm acting like an idiot."

"You're acting like a woman who knows she's wanted…and isn't real pleased with the idea. You're acting like a smart lady."

Tess wanted to laugh. When had she ever been smart where Jake Walker was concerned? She was running on instinct alone, not the rules she normally lived by. And her instincts had always been woefully inadequate. They'd betrayed her in the past.

She cast a sideways glance at Jake. "I'm an engaged woman," she said softly and with conviction. "Gray's a good man."

Jake studied her for one long moment, his dangerous eyes concealed by dark sunglasses, hiding his expression. Then he nodded slowly. "Gray always set a fine example for those around him, and you don't have to worry that I'll forget that or anything else. I've given up attempted theft these days." He turned from her, ignoring her quick intake of breath. "You'll make a fine mayor's wife, Tess."

The road before her became a blur. Tess pulled over to the side. She turned to Jake.

"I never meant to sound like I was accusing you of anything."

She hadn't. There was no reason to. She was the one who had carried a crush for Jake all those years ago when the man hadn't even known she existed. And for all his suggestive comments those first few days at his house, he'd shown her respect. Wasn't she the one who had lost control the other day? Wasn't it she who, by her very expression, had invited his kiss? Wasn't he the one who had pulled away?

Her words of warning had been for herself, not for him. He'd just assured her that he wouldn't seduce her. She wasn't going to have him thinking that she thought him a liar.

Jake shook his head, his lips turned up slightly. "If you weren't accusing me, you should have been. You're an intensely desirable woman, Tess. I'd have to be ninety-nine percent dead not to want to make love to you, so even if you had been accusing me of lust, I wouldn't have been offended. As it is, I'm just assuring you that I'll do my best to control my baser urges. With a little luck, I'll be able to hold out until we're able to finish up here. You're safe, Tess."

What a whopper of a lie. No way was she safe, not from her thoughts. His presence awakened irrepressible and uncomfortable desires in her. At night she dreamed of things that didn't even exist and had never existed.

Tess sighed with unease. Fumbling to slide the shift into Drive, she pulled back onto the empty street. By reminding Jake and herself that she was engaged, she'd hoped to pull things back into their nice neat slots, the way she liked her world. She'd hoped to reset the scene and regain control of her tumultuous emotions.

But now she could see that only Jake's absence could rid her of her unresolved adolescent fantasies. Once he was away from here, she would return to normal. She would.

"All right. Sit back and hold on, Jake," she finally managed to say. "We're going to take the whirlwind tour of the building industry. By the time we get back today, you're going to know more about general contractors than you ever wanted to know."

And she was going to be that much closer to fulfilling her duties for the committee, that much closer to contributing something worthwhile to her town and being a credit to Grayson and his career. Jake would be that much nearer to being gone.

The lady knew her stuff, all right. Jake had been traveling around with her for hours and he hadn't failed to notice that she was personally acquainted with every contractor they spoke to. She asked about their families. She knew the histories of the homes they were working on and the ones they had built five years ago.

She was an impressive lady, and one who was in control. Usually. True, he'd made her nervous back there in the car. It had seemed almost cruel to remind her of the chemistry that bubbled between them whenever they got close, especially when she was so obviously committed to Gray Alexander, and when he himself knew better than to give in to the hot steady thrum of arousal she called up in him.

But she was so clearly a woman who played by the rules, it had only been fair to let her see the cards he held, to let her know that he had a potentially dangerous hand. That way Tess could build her defenses and be ready in case he began to get too close. He had been trying to reassure her, but also to warn her. He'd spent years harnessing his urges, not giving in, but there was just something about the lady that pushed the borders of his self-control. He wanted her to be prepared to slap his face if he stepped out of line. He was trusting her to do so.

Still, right now she looked almost incapable of the slightest movement. Falling back into the car seat, she let out a breath.

"That was the last one, thank goodness. I'm sorry. I guess I underestimated just how long this would take. Are you ready for me to take you home?"

She looked like a wilted flower, lying there on the seat. Limp but beautiful, trying to maintain a smile, to continue to be ornamental when she was clearly too tired to do anything other than breathe.

Jake shook his head.

Her eyes opened wide. "So no one seemed just right? I was thinking maybe of Tony Bushnell. He's very detail-conscious and he has a great deal of experience with old houses. Or maybe Bryan Clydell. He's young but he's incredibly easy to work with. If neither of them suits you, I'm not sure—"

"Shh." Jake reached out, gently soothing two fingers over her eyelids. Her eyes fluttered closed.

"Either of those men would be fine, Tess. I merely meant that you don't need to take me home. I'll drive, you've had enough."

She looked up at him, opened her mouth to protest, but he was already opening the door and taking her hand to assist her around to the passenger side. "No arguments, Tess, I told you I wanted to have a look at this car. Now is as good a time as any."

Her brows drew together in a frown. "I told you I'd research it."

He smiled, gently urging her into the car. "That could

take a while, and as someone once told me, I can make the whole process much more efficient for you. I know my cars, Tess.''

"It's just a car.''

"Cars can be dangerous. They need care.''

"You don't have to do this.''

"And you don't have to help me, either, but you are.'' Jake paused, wondering how to shut up those beautiful lips of hers. He could kiss her, but then he'd promised he wouldn't do that. She'd never want him to do that. "I don't like to feel I owe anyone anything, Tess. Helping you will feel like I'm repaying my debts.''

She looked up at him, out of eyes as intense and violet as a coastal sunset. Then suddenly she nodded. Barely. But still she'd accepted his terms.

Something shifted inside Jake. He felt marginally better than he had a few seconds earlier. Just slightly, and he knew he would have rather tasted her lips. But at least he'd won her cooperation.

He was just opening his door when the sound of angry cries caught his attention. Pausing, he looked down the street. A small knot of boys was visible at the far end of the block. A living, breathing knot. A mess of arms and legs and fists. Laughter. Heat. Loud voices. Angry voices? Was this a kid's game? An impromptu wrestling match? Probably. He should leave it alone, and yet— Jake studied the scene, the wisdom of messing in something he knew nothing of. Until he saw the kid lying on the ground in the middle of that circle of faces. Until he saw the boy wince.

"Stay here,'' he ordered Tess without waiting for her reply.

In only seconds he was down the street. A few seconds more he had ordered the mob to disband. He was examining the boy's arms and legs for breaks. The left eye would be black, there were scratches on the kid's face and his nose was bleeding slightly, but his limbs were intact. As far as Jake could tell his injuries would hurt but they were not life-threatening. Not this time at least.

Jake turned to face the crowd he'd dispersed. From the distance they'd looked older, but this child in front of him was just that. A child. Maybe ten, possibly eleven. No older. The rest were just the same.

"Want to explain?" he asked the boy who'd been at the center of the fray.

The child looked up at him through tough, stubborn eyes. He remained silent.

"He rode off on my bicycle and broke the light," another boy yelled.

"He did. I saw him." The voice came from behind Jake who didn't turn or even look away from the bruised and accused child in front of him.

The boy still didn't speak, but he didn't drop his gaze from Jake's, either.

Jake recognized that look, he'd lived with that look. For years. In the mirror. Every day.

The boy wasn't denying his accusers, he wasn't defending himself, but then he wouldn't do that, even if he was innocent. Jake knew that was true. He knew it as well as he knew anything at all.

"Did you..." He hesitated, knowing his tone was very important here. "Did you take the bicycle?" he asked. There were witnesses. By rights the question should have been not "did you?" but "why did you?" But the whys weren't always easy. He knew that much.

The boy with the old, old eyes stared at him unblinkingly, arrogant even when he'd been caught. "What do you think?"

Jake studied him, ignoring the other boys' jeers. "I think that if you did take it, it probably wouldn't have been as satisfying as you might have thought. I once took a model car that didn't belong to me. It was shiny and red and I thought that having it would make me happy, but—" He held out his hands as if searching for the right words. "But instead, it didn't make me happy. It was just a thing, and it wasn't really mine, anyway. Every time I looked at it, I felt...ugly inside. I finally buried it, but that didn't make me feel any better."

The boy let the silence slip in. "So what did you do?" he asked at last.

"I dug it up, I cleaned it up, and left it on the boy's porch. The one I had taken it from."

"Did he know that you took it?"

"I don't know. Probably. He never said."

"Did you feel better then?"

"A little. Not great, but better."

The boy stared at the bicycle lying behind the crowd. "The light's broken. Smashed," he admitted.

"You could replace it."

He shook his head. "No money."

Jake wanted to walk away. He wished he'd never gotten involved in all this. "You could get a job, help me fix up that car down there." He motioned back to Tess's car—and noticed that the lady had slipped up beside him. She was watching him with almost as much interest as this pack of young wolves. "Ask your parents if you could come work out at the Walker place for a day. One day's work should be enough to pay for a broken bicycle light."

The boy nodded, Jake started to walk away, but the

boy whose bicycle had been stolen ran up beside him. "How do you know he'll come? How do you know he'll fix my bike?"

Jake stared down at the irate kid. He had a valid question.

"This is a small town. I'll know if he doesn't. Most of all, *he'll* know if he doesn't. You'll get your bike fixed within the week. I guarantee it."

The boy with the bike looked uncertain. "I don't know you. My dad—"

"I'll talk to your father, Danny," Tess stepped in. "If Mr. Walker says your bike will be repaired, then it will be."

Tess had meant her words to reassure, but when the boys had gone, Jake speared her with his gaze. "Be careful what you promise on my behalf, Tess. You don't know me much better than they do."

It was true, all too true, but somehow she *did* know him. She trusted him. She could have said that she'd replace the broken light herself, but that wasn't what she'd meant at all.

"It was good of you to offer Paul an honest way to work off the cost. He's been in a lot of trouble lately," she said gently. "His father doesn't pay much attention to him. The family doesn't have much money. He must have wanted a bike badly—"

"Don't excuse the kid," Jake said, cutting her off. "He stole, he committed a crime, and he knows it. But it wasn't a *bike* that he wanted."

Furrowing her brow, Tess looked up at Jake, confused.

His laugh was low and without humor. "It was a feeling, sweet Tess. He thought that having that bike would make him feel something he wanted to feel. Too bad he didn't get to run with it long enough to realize he was wrong.''

"But that story you told him—"

"Was no story, Tess. At least not most of it. And it won't have the least bit of effect on him. He'll have to find those things out himself. He isn't about to believe me just because I say so. But maybe a day's work, a little praise and the chance to repay what he's taken will give him just a touch of that feeling he was looking for. Just a hint of pride.''

He held out his hand as if to take hers, but then let it fall back to his side. "Come on, I've got to figure out what's wrong with your car if I've got a mechanic's helper coming. If I'm going to give him work, I need to know what in hell the job entails.''

She smiled up at him, walking back to the car at his side. In the space of five minutes, Jake had just gotten more complicated, more dangerous. She wanted to paint him innocent, but he kept coming up with truths that pointed to his total lack of innocence. She wanted to keep him at a distance, but everything he did and said and was kept pulling her closer.

She watched him as he drove, his hands sure and strong on the oversize wheel of her old car. He never turned her way, but she was almost certain that he knew she was watching him.

"You talked of pride, but I saw that scrapbook, Jake. Your mother was very proud of you.'' She'd said that before, but after looking at that book, she could say it with more conviction.

Jake shook his head, smiled. "She loved me, and she was proud, but I let her down.''

"When you were expelled.''

"My happiness and success was all she ever wanted.''

"She would have forgiven you."

Jake slowed, turned to Tess. "She never held it against me, Tess. Never held any of it against me. When I came home that day and she immediately absolved me of blame, I knew it was time to go. She was a good and talented and loving lady, but in this town she was just Jake Walker's mother. When I left, she became her own woman. People began to see her for the wonderful lady she was."

Tess wanted to reach over and shake him. If he hadn't been driving she wasn't sure she wouldn't have done just that.

"But she was alone, Jake. She missed you. And don't tell me you wrote, you called. I know all that."

Jake pulled up in front of her house and killed the engine.

"She'd spent her whole life loving me. In spite of everything, Tess. Forgiving me for anything. It was time to show her how much I loved *her*."

"But you left her."

"Yes." He didn't say more, and she knew she wasn't going to win this battle. He had left his mother because he loved her, because he wanted her to have a chance to shine without the cloud of his past hanging over her. That was all. He wouldn't have it any other way.

Tess wanted to argue, to tell him he should have stayed. But she couldn't. Flora Walker *had* shone, she had been happy in her own way. And Jake would have been miserable in this town. He was convinced that he had done what was best for his mother.

She held out her hands in defeat, turned to open her door.

"I'll make a decision on the contractor in the next day or two, Tess," Jake promised. "And, Tess?"

Turning, she looked back over her shoulder straight into his eyes. "Yes?"

He nodded toward her tree, the one she loved to look at out her window in the morning. "Have you done any more research on that situation?"

His gaze was unwavering, he was waiting for an answer.

Tess gave a guilty shrug. "I'll get to it in the next few days. I have students, and your house—"

"Damn the house, Tess, and damn your students, too. I'll bet they don't have trees falling down on their heads. You're getting up early in the morning?"

She blinked at this sudden change of subject. "I—Jake?"

He swore again under his breath. "Of course you are. You wake the blasted sun up every morning, don't you? Well, tomorrow, be prepared for company, Tess. I have a strong urge to pound something. It might as well be that branch. You'll have a good supply of wood when the day is done."

Tess took a breath, she opened her eyes wider. "Jake, that's not necessary. You're not—"

"Watch me, lady." He leaned closer over her seat, his lips hovering near her own. "Be up and dressed at sunrise, sweetheart. It's your turn to have uninvited company. Don't make any other plans."

He was nearly on top of her, then gone just as quickly.

As Tess dressed for bed that night, she told herself that she was dreading the morning.

But she knew that she lied. She also knew enough not to pay any attention to her feelings. She had gotten over Jake once before, she would easily do so again.

But first he had to go.

First she had to get through the next day.

Chapter Seven

The day was muggy, the branch was a bigger son of a gun up close than it had looked from his vantage point across the street, and in the end Jake had to resort to an elaborate scheme of ropes and pulleys just to keep the darn thing from toppling onto Tess's roof while he removed it.

But that was okay. Heck, it was better than okay, because concentrating on the work kept his mind off the woman on the ground below.

Tess was hovering around looking worried, as if she thought he might come crashing down on his keister at any moment.

"Are you sure you don't want me to go get someone to help you?" she called.

Jake chuckled. It was the third time she'd asked that same question in the last ten minutes.

"Don't worry, the hardest part's done, Tess," he assured her. "Everything's secure. Now all I have to do is take this puppy down and lower it to the ground."

Readying himself to do just that, he wiped the back of his hand across his forehead. The bandanna he'd wound around his head earlier was damp, his long hair brushed against his bare shoulders. A trickle of sweat slipped down his spine. It was hot as heck in this tree, but despite his reassurances to Tess, he couldn't afford to rush things now. The darned log was heavy as all get-out, and he was perched on a branch a good twenty feet off the ground.

"Okay, Tess," he said, glancing down at her. "I want you to do me a favor now."

Her hair swung back as she tipped her face up to him and finally managed a smile of relief. He wondered what she'd say if she knew just how much of the sweet curve of her breasts was revealed by the innocent vee of her blouse when a man was staring down at her from above.

He frowned at his totally inappropriate thought and Tess tilted her head, losing her own smile.

"Is something wrong? Can I help you after all, Jake?"

"You can help me by moving out from under this tree, darlin'. Right now. The end of this branch is hanging over your house, but the lion's share is right above your precious little head. I'd rather not take the risk of you getting hurt, so move away now. Back by the fence would be just about perfect."

The moment of truth had come and he could see that Tess wasn't at all certain that he could do this alone, but she did move away. Slowly and with obvious reluctance.

Tugging up the cuff on his glove, Jake unclipped the chain saw from the belt he had fastened around his waist. He checked his lines, then turned on the motor and laid the blade to the branch. The wood sliced easily, like butter that had been sitting out on a hot day. The lines caught the weight of the heavy limb and held it fast as Jake cut the power on the saw and began his descent.

When he got to the ground, he waved Tess away. "Just let me get this baby down safely," he told her.

He sensed rather than saw Tess's nod. "You've done this before," she said softly, and sometime later as she watched him from a distance.

As the troublesome branch came to rest on the ground, Jake let go of the rope, let his taut muscles go slack and finally allowed himself to look at Tess. He was sweat-soaked and slick while she looked like a spring breeze in her white shorts and blouse. He wondered what it would be like to cool his hot body against her own, then immediately rejected even the thought.

Jake shrugged. "I moved around a lot and learned to do a number of things after I left Misunderstood. It's how I got started writing how-to's in a way. I became a jack-of-all-trades."

She nodded and began walking his way as he knelt on one knee to disentangle the lines that still held the branch.

"You were probably right about that branch, you know," she said, eyeing the monster piece of wood. "I'm grateful for your help, but really, you don't have to bother breaking it up. Now that it's on the ground it's no danger. You need a rest and definitely something cool. I'll just be a minute. Sit down." She waved her hand toward an area set deep into the yard and graced by several comfortable-looking summer chairs.

Her comment about something cool too closely mirrored his thoughts just a few seconds before and Jake nearly groaned, but he forced himself to concentrate on the last line she'd spoken. "If you think I'm leaving here without splitting this wood for you, then I didn't make myself clear earlier. Besides, aren't you always teaching your students that labor is good for the soul? Believe me, I split my share of wood as a kid and it's definitely not just work. It's therapy. I should be paying you for the chance to do this.''

He was teasing her, smiling at her, but in truth he wasn't exactly lying. Tess had moved closer to talk to him and now she was near enough that he could smell the light honeysuckle, woman scent of her. When he'd looked back through her yard, he'd been unable to ignore the wide free-standing hammock that was moving in the breeze. He'd noticed it earlier, had wondered if Tess ever slept there on hot, summer nights. He'd envisioned her there with her hair spread out against the cool cotton canvas and he'd tried not to think of himself lying there with her. No matter, Jake didn't want to set foot in that direction. He definitely didn't want to go anywhere remotely near that hammock when Tess was around.

"I'm darn well going to chop this wood for you," he repeated, wondering if his words were more for himself or for Tess.

But it wouldn't have mattered. She'd already gone. She'd disappeared right inside her house. Good. Real good.

Tess fluttered around inside her house, and "fluttered" was exactly the word to describe what she was doing, she decided. The thought didn't sit well with her, but watching Jake this morning had put a definite strain on her nerves. Watching him work, so deft and sure of himself, so obviously strong when he'd finally shed his shirt in the morning's heat, it had been all she could do to try to appear natural and calm when calm wasn't at all what she was feeling.

His jeans hung low on his hips, revealing smooth, tanned skin. The muscles in his forearms flexed with every movement, and with that bandanna holding back that mane of black hair of his that brushed his shoulder with every movement, Jake looked somewhat...wild, a totally sensual animal. There was the dragon, and a small scar high on his chest he'd earned somehow in the last eleven years. Tess wanted to know how he got it. She'd been unable to tear her gaze away.

Staring up at him, Tess had felt...wanton. She was no longer just a teacher, just a local businesswoman, no longer the very proper woman she'd always been. For the first time in her life she was letting her hormones get away with her the way she'd known other people to do—and the out-of-control sensation was just... unacceptable.

But there was more to this shaky feeling coursing inside her than just animal lust, and that was even worse. Tess knew that as she sliced lemons, squeezed them and measured out sugar for lemonade. The problem was that with Jake's insinuation into her own backyard, into her own affairs, she could no longer tell herself that he was just a man she was helping, that theirs was strictly a business arrangement. She was no longer just admiring Jake from afar in an innocent fashion. She was letting him into her life and no way was that supposed to happen.

But it had. There he was in her yard, chopping her wood, and damn it, she couldn't very well send him away without at least giving the man something to drink before he left.

Carefully, she placed glasses and the pitcher of lemonade on a tray. Then she took three deep breaths and prepared to go face Jake again.

He had found a clear spot of ground. One length he'd cut was already standing on end as he readied himself to split it.

"Couldn't you just use the saw?" Tess asked, eyeing the single-edged ax Jake had brought with him.

Jake's grin was broad. He swung the ax high, and brought it down with a resounding clump against the wood, which flew apart in two neat halves. "Definitely, I could do that," he said, pausing to look at her. "Just the way people could drive everywhere instead of bothering to jog. But besides the exercise value, there's something eminently satisfying about the grunt value of chopping wood the old-fashioned way. My mother used to send me out regularly to chop wood when I needed to let off steam." He picked up another length of wood, braced his feet wide and brought down the ax again.

"Smart lady," Tess conceded, moving nearer with the pitcher of lemonade. She could see the long streaks of perspiration slipping down his backbone, and her breath caught in her throat.

"Maybe…maybe you should take a break for a minute," she said, holding out the tray of lemonade. "I've already put the ice in the glasses."

He looked down to where she held the tray in front of her like a shield and for a moment she thought he was going to refuse her offer. Then he nodded once, tightly, and allowed her to lead the way back to the table.

Setting the tray down, she busied herself pouring the lemonade, trying to convince herself that the crackle of the ice as the liquid flowed over it was louder than the thundering of her heart. But when she looked up to see if Jake had heard anything unusual, he wasn't looking at her at all. His gaze was firmly fixed on the hammock she'd lain on last night watching the stars.

Tess swallowed hard. She passed him his glass, making sure her fingers didn't touch his own.

"What was your mother like?" he asked suddenly, looking her directly in the eyes.

Startled, Tess blinked hard. "Excuse me?"

"Sorry," he said sheepishly, "but we've talked about my mother before. What about you? What was your life like as a kid? I know you didn't start out here in Misunderstood."

She stared at him momentarily, watched as he raised his glass to his lips. "No. No, I didn't," she whispered. "I grew up in Indiana and my mother was...beautiful, highly intelligent...sad." Tess shook her head and looked away. "I think it must have been very hard for her living with a man who told her he loved her again and again and then proved that it was a lie on a regular basis."

Tess hesitated, then took a deep breath. "My father was a complete philanderer, not a man a woman could trust. My ex-husband was much the same," she said, marveling at the fact that she was even making that statement. But her words had been a warning, to Jake and to herself. She knew that. They were meant to put some distance between them.

She looked up at him and found him gazing down at her fiercely.

He reached out, and stroked two long fingers down the side of her face. "I always pictured you living in perpetual sunshine," he whispered, his voice a caress filled with deep concern.

Tess swallowed hard. She shook her head tightly, then forced a smile, trying to ignore the feel of his fingertips as they grazed a sensitive spot just beneath her jaw. "No one lives in perpetual sunshine, Jake, and I've finally found the life I was meant for. I'm happy now."

"I'm glad," he said, slipping his hand away. "Real glad. I wouldn't want to think of you any other way."

The utter conviction in his tone nearly undid Tess. "And you've got the life you want, too, don't you?" she asked. "You like California?"

He shrugged, smiled briefly. "What's not to like, Tess? Doesn't everyone love the ocean, the mountains, a temperate climate?"

Placing his glass on the table, he turned from her, moved to make his way back to his work. There was still a substantial task ahead, but as she stared at the proud, determined line of his spine, as she watched him draw himself to his full height, intent on doing his good deed for her, Tess knew she had been pushed to her limit. Jake's voice had been firm when he'd insisted that he was happy with his life, but his smile had been too practiced, too smooth. She was wondering about him, worrying about him, and now she was going to have to spend more hours watching him slave with his muscles for her.

"Don't." Impulsively she reached out and touched the back of his arm, her damp fingertips meeting warm male skin.

He turned, sending her hopping back two steps, nearly stumbling.

Jake slipped his arm around her waist and walked her back to a stand. Now the hammock was only a few feet behind them.

"Don't what?" he whispered, but Tess was beyond thought now. All she could register was the steely strength of Jake around her, the warm male scent of him surrounding her, the need to press her lips to the bare skin so close to her mouth.

"Don't," she simply repeated, but there was no conviction in her whispery voice. None. The word sounded almost like a promise, like an invitation.

Jake moved slightly, sweeping her closer. "Tess," he said, his voice hoarse and strangled. "I'm sorry, Tess."

And then his mouth was on hers, he held her close in his arms, cupped her head with his big palm.

His touch was dark magic, drugging, hungry...and she wanted to be closer. She wanted him never to stop.

Tess slid one hand into the dark silk of his hair. She rested the other on his chest, felt the thud of his heartbeat beneath her fingers. Closing her eyes and her mind, she gave in to the feel of his lips brushing her own, she opened her mouth beneath his when he urged her to.

If she could have twined herself closer to him, she would have. She was on the verge of wrapping herself around him completely when a gust of wind whipped something against the backs of her legs.

The startling feel of something other than Jake's touch made Tess stiffen. She froze in Jake's arms, registering his deep intake of breath as he steadied her on her feet and set her away from him.

Raising her head, Tess realized that they had moved backward, they were nearly on the hammock. In another moment they would have been, and she knew without question that this would have been no one-sided event. She would have been beyond stopping, would have gladly fallen with Jake onto the rough fabric and given in to the desire that had been shaking her world ever since he'd arrived in town.

"Tess." His voice was an apology, clearly an apology.

"Don't say it," she managed to choke out. "Don't you dare take all the blame. It was me, too. The day, this setting, it was..."

"It was damn good, totally wonderful, and it's not going to happen ever again. I don't want you doing the confession scene with Gray in order to punish yourself. If anything needs saying, I'll tell him just what happened, that I tried to seduce you."

Tess couldn't stop the gasp from escaping her lips. With longing still pervading her body, fierce feelings of guilt rocked her. But Jake had not seduced her, and she was not going to allow him to take the blame.

"It was an accident," she said stubbornly.

Jake looked her dead in the eye and shook his head. "Maybe it was an 'accident' for you, Tess, but not for me. The word accident implies something that a person never meant to happen, and I've been thinking about kissing you just like this since the minute I saw you crossing the road that first day. Now I've done it, and it won't happen again. But it wasn't anything close to an accident."

There was finality in his voice. He turned and began to walk away.

"And don't touch this wood or try to move it yourself," he said, snagging his shirt on one finger as he moved toward the front of her yard. "I'll finish this when you're away from home, but don't look for me tomorrow. I need a day to cool down and get some things done. And, Tess?"

She took a deep breath as he turned to look at her one more time. All she could manage was a nod.

"It was just as sweet as I knew it would be. The best. And I'm not really sorry. My fault, sweetheart. Don't lose any sleep feeling guilty. Gray would understand. He knows what I'm like.''

She wanted to argue with him, to do something childish like stamp her foot and tell him that she was perfectly capable of kissing him without feeling guilty. She considered telling him that she had wanted to kiss him all along, too, and she had now gotten him out of *her* system.

But she did none of those things. Responsibility was buried deep inside her. She did not act childish when she could help it...and she did not lie.

It wouldn't have mattered, anyway. Jake was already gone and all that was left was the sound of the swinging gate. Tess wondered how many other women besides her and Cassie had heard that gate swinging shut in their dreams. She wondered if she would ever be able to forget Jake's kiss while lying in Gray's arms.

Jake was as good as his word. He didn't come around for the rest of that day or all of the next.

Annoyed with herself for her lack of discipline and her unforgivable disregard for Gray, the mindless way she'd melted into Jake's arms and had practically invited him to kiss her, Tess attempted to drive away her demons by knuckling under and getting some work done. She made lesson plans that didn't need to be made for another six weeks. She cut out letters for bulletin boards and displays and searched through manuals for fresh and creative new teaching ideas. She scrubbed every wall in her house, every floor, every bathroom and kitchen fixture. She went for long walks, walks upon walks.

But she couldn't ignore the fact that while she had been gone Jake had, indeed, finished chopping her wood and had stacked it neatly at the side of her house.

She couldn't help noticing the book on butterfly gardening that was left on her doorstep, wrapped in paper. "For all your trouble" the message on the flyleaf said, and she didn't have to ask who had left the book. She didn't have to wonder who had delivered the pots of pinks and hollyhocks that were labeled "attracts painted ladies" or those of red and white phlox whose tags indicated that they were alluring to tiger swallowtails and red admirals.

She tried to ignore the fact that the man was still too close to forget, but Tess was all too aware that Jake was at the back of his house, pulling away loose boards. She couldn't help but see when Tony Bushnell stopped by and began to take his own measurements, and she wondered if Jake had agreed to hire the man to draw up his plans.

But she didn't ask and she didn't venture near. She didn't even argue when Paul, the boy who had stolen the bicycle, arrived the next morning and asked if he could have her keys so he and Mr. Walker could work on her car. She simply handed them over and watched the boy race back to Jake's house. She merely tried to ignore the sounds of the boy and man as Jake explained what they were going to do and Paul's silence slowly began to give way to talk and laughter.

Several hours later, he was back, keys in hand.

"Thank you so much, Paul," she said, noting the look of pure satisfaction on his face.

"It's all fixed, Ms. Buchanan. Mr. Walker showed me how to figure out what was wrong. I think we've stopped that pinging sound. Changed your oil and spark plugs while we were at it. It's running like a breeze now."

Tess's smile widened. She'd never heard Paul speak

that many words in a row in all of her memory. She'd very rarely seen him smile.

"Then I'm glad, Paul. I'll feel much safer driving now when I go into town," she assured him. "Hold on just a minute and I'll get my purse."

Paul's brow bunched into a frown as he shook his head. "No way, Ms. Buchanan. Mr. Walker already paid me enough to take care of the light I broke and a little bit more besides. I don't want anyone thinking I was trying to mooch some more money off you. I just brought back your keys like he asked me to."

Tess's eyebrows rose. "I see. Well, thank you, Paul. I appreciate your hard work."

She closed the door as he walked away, waiting until he was far down the street. Then she opened the door again. Jake was taking this too far. He'd removed a dangerous branch for her, chopped her wood, delivered a book and plants she hadn't paid for, and now he had paid Paul for working on *her* car, not to mention the work he himself had put into the task. No way was she going to let this kind of thing continue and she intended to go over there, thank him, and very firmly let him know that he had done enough right this minute.

Tess stepped out onto the porch. She took two steps down the stairs to the ground. She looked toward her destination. A picture of Jake staring down into her eyes just before he kissed her rose unwilled and unwanted into her consciousness…and she froze completely.

He'd said that he needed a day to cool down. He'd said that she shouldn't look for him today, but hadn't she been looking for him all day? Hadn't she been waiting for him to come to her and kiss her again?

No. No, she hadn't. The denial whirled through Tess's mind like a tornado on the loose. She didn't want Jake to kiss her, and she didn't want to hurt Gray. In fact, she couldn't wait to become Mrs. Gray Alexander, and she didn't intend to get within touching distance of Jake again. The mere stroke of his hand confused her. It made her think irrational thoughts, dream irrelevant dreams.

No way did she want that. The past was still clear in her mind, and she was not going to be the next Cassie Pratt, mindless with need for the wrong kind of man.

Backing up slowly, Tess quietly slipped back into her house, shutting the door firmly, proud of herself. She had resisted temptation and the powerful lure of Jake.

So when Gray called and asked her to meet him for dinner just a few hours later, she was able to do so with a sense of anticipation. Gray was a good man, she was a lucky woman.

And when Gray told her that Jake had left a message for the committee acknowledging that he would have preliminary plans that he would like to submit for review in only a few days, Tess was able to take a deep breath and agree that she was glad they were finally going to get things settled with the house, that things would soon settle down to what they had been before Jake came to town.

She was able to beat back the tiny twinge of hurt that Jake had not called her with the news.

"I have to say I'm glad you won't have to be working with him too much longer, sunshine," Gray said. "The guy rubs me the wrong way."

Tess shook her head as Gray took her hand in his own and kissed her fingers apologetically for talking so much about work. "It won't be long before you'll forget he was ever even in town," she assured her fiancé.

And she would feel the same way, Tess told herself. She swore she'd forget Jake the second he was gone.

Chapter Eight

Two days had passed. No, three, Jake mused, staring out his window. And all of them had been hell.

He'd done his best to shove Tess and the unexpected honey of her lips right out of his mind, but his good intentions had been just that. Something he intended to do, something he knew he should do, hell, even something he wanted to do, but couldn't.

He'd known all along that she was there, moving in and out of her house, and he was so damned glad that he would be leaving in a couple of days. Then the wondering and worrying about her would stop.

Then she would be strictly Gray's business—for life.

Jake looked down at the long, rolled piece of paper on the table in front of him. Tomorrow the Historical Preservation Committee would meet and review the plans he'd had drawn up. He'd doubled Tony's fee to get him to do them in a rush. Once the committee okayed the drawings—and Tony assured him there would be no problem—there'd be no reason to stay any longer. Jake had seen Tony's work, he'd checked his record. The man would see to it that everything got done as planned, and Jake could handle any questions or problems over the phone. Since he didn't intend to live in the house, he had no intention of being overly fussy.

Flattening his palms on the table, Jake looked around the room. It was old, it was crumbling, and there were a lot of unpleasant memories, but…there had been happier moments, sweet ones that had paled in his memory. They'd been fleeting in his childhood and overshadowed by the bigger, uglier times. No matter what he'd done or become, he and his mother had shared so much. She *had* known how much he cared for her. Looking through the scrapbook of photos Tess had returned to him, he'd remembered. He'd been forced to remember that there had been love in this house and that it had not all been one-sided.

She'd written notes, brief messages on pale blue slips of paper that she'd pressed between the pages of the book. Tess had done that, the woman who had befriended his mother and who had made this house her quest. The woman he'd kissed until they were both dizzy and senseless and not thinking at all, had almost more of a stake in this house than he did. And he hadn't even let her see the plans.

Would she want to? Yes, of course. Hell, no, probably not if it meant being too near to him again. Heck, he didn't know, not at all. But he ought to at least ask. He should at least give her that courtesy.

Snatching up the architect's scroll before he could change his mind, Jake moved out, hit the screen door with the flat of his palm, sending it bouncing outward as he headed for Tess.

She was sitting on her porch swing, a textbook in her

hand. As he neared her steps, Jake knew he couldn't go up there. The hard, flat slats of the swing looked too inviting. He'd be much too tempted to sit down beside her and pull her onto his lap.

He could see her take a deep breath as she put the book down beside her and came to the edge of the porch. She was barefoot and the nakedness of her skin invited his gaze to crawl higher. Up her long legs to where cherry red shorts hid his view. Over the white cotton blouse with the V neck that revealed her pale throat. Raising his glance just a notch, Jake quickly forced his gaze not to linger on those lips that he remembered all too well. Instead he went straight for those lovely eyes that were looking back at him, wide and confused.

"Gray said you'd be leaving soon." Her voice was nearly a whisper. "I guess I'll see you at the meeting tomorrow."

Damn, she was dismissing him.

"Definitely," he agreed, "but it didn't seem fair, somehow, making you wait to see the plans when you've put so much of yourself into this project. You're the one who got it off the ground."

"No." She started to shake her head, but Jake raised one eyebrow.

"You're not the lady that marched up to my door and threatened to tear my house down with her bare hands?"

A small smile lifted Tess's lips. "At least I didn't threaten to huff and puff and blow it down."

Jake looked over his shoulder toward his house. "There are probably parts of the house where a strong wind might do the trick, but what I'm saying, Tess, is that you deserve to see these plans before anyone else does. I would have shown them to you already, but—"

She raised one hand. "I know. Don't say it."

Jake knew she was right. It was probably better not to even talk about what had happened the other day. He knew that for all that she'd responded, probably *because* she'd responded to his touch, she was regretting that moment in time. She was thinking that she was another Cassie. He wished, really wished, that for once he could tell her the truth, but he couldn't do that. He couldn't sacrifice Cassie and her boy for his own selfish purposes.

"Anyway," he continued. "I wondered if you wanted to look at these." He held out the rolled-up plans. "You'll see them tomorrow, of course."

"But it wouldn't be the same, would it?" she asked. "Thank you—for thinking of me—and for all the other. The tree, the plants, my car."

Jake frowned. "There's no need to thank me, and anyway, you already did. I got your note. Paul shared the brownies you gave him this morning and he told me that you insisted on paying him for delivery services. He wasn't sure if he should have taken it considering that it was just a piece of paper and that I live just across the street."

And why in hell had he used that word? "Live"? He didn't live here, he was just passing through.

Tess smiled and shook her head impatiently. "I know, but it wasn't that much, and I did appreciate him taking the trouble to run it over when it was obvious that he was eager to be off to tell his dad that you'd agreed to let him help you tune up your bike."

Blowing out a breath, Jake's eyebrows drew together. "I probably shouldn't have let him do that. Bikes can be dangerous."

"He told me that they were," she said gently. "He also told me that he liked your bike a lot but what he really wanted was a Ferrari someday. He hoped you wouldn't be insulted. It's been rough for him since his mother left and his father was forced into a lower-paying position with all those long hours. His father's a good man, but Paul's been living in a shell lately. He's gotten into trouble. If you hadn't come by the other day, things would have—''

''Been fine,'' Jake provided. He didn't want any misconceptions about his motives. ''It's too easy for a kid to let his anger get the best of him and turn him down the wrong road, but I don't think that would have happened with Paul. When I talked to his father, Ray told me that he hadn't been able to spend as much time with his son because of the crazy shifts he's been working. That's going to change soon. Paul knows things will be back to normal then. He would have been fine no matter what.''

''But the attention you gave him *now* made a difference,'' Tess insisted, crossing her arms and giving him that ultrasexy, firm look that made him want to touch her to see if she would bend and flow into his arms.

''Want to look at my drawings, Ms. Buchanan?'' he whispered, trying to change the subject.

Tess blew out a breath, she uncrossed her arms. ''Do butterflies like lilac bushes?'' she asked. ''Come on.'' She motioned toward her house.

Instant alarms went off in Jake's head. Her house was way too private, his, too. He hadn't been near her for more than five minutes and already his hands were itching to touch her, to stroke Tess, another man's woman.

''I've got a sudden strong urge to see the public park in the center of town,'' he told her.

''Public park?'' Confusion furrowed Tess's brow, and then the light dawned. ''You're right,'' she agreed. ''There are picnic tables there we can spread the plans out on. It's a good day for the park. A good day for a *walk*," she added, and Jake knew she didn't want to sit behind him on his cycle or be closed up with him in her car.

"Damn good day for a walk," he agreed, resisting the urge to take her hand as she slipped on her shoes and came down the steps to join him.

He knew he should ask about Gray, but he didn't. He couldn't be *that* generous. He was attracted to Tess and he didn't want to be. *She* didn't want him to be, but he'd be damned if he'd go so far as to make small talk about the man who would get to share the rest of her days.

"Catch any butterflies?" he asked instead.

She smiled up at him, her movement causing her hand to bump his side. Carefully she moved six inches away. "They're starting to come around," she admitted. "I just hope those lovely flowers can survive my brown thumb."

"You can always plant a border of marigolds up your walkway. They're good, too, and hardy," he offered. But the silence set in after his comment. By the time the next spring planting time came, she would be living somewhere else. Gray had a rolling expanse of grass in front of his house, with no walkway. Jake hadn't been able to stop himself from driving by to look at the place Tess would call home soon.

"I do like marigolds," Tess finally said softly. "They don't smell nice, but they're so cheerful and bright."

Jake did take her hand then. He squeezed it just once, lightly, then let it go. "I'll think of you surrounded by butterflies when I'm back in California," he said. "You have a lot in common with your little friends. You make the world a richer place."

She started to thank him, or maybe to protest, but then she turned away without speaking.

They walked down the streets of Misunderstood as the heat-soaked concrete warmed the soles of their shoes and Jake marveled at how much more he enjoyed walking through this town than he ever had before. It didn't matter that they weren't talking. She was with him...for now.

He'd just turned to stare down at her again when he felt it, that familiar feeling that he was being watched.

Jake looked to the right and saw Dora Averly, his former teacher, being helped out the door of Bickerson's Drugs by Craig. The woman had paused dead center of the door, leaving it gaping as Craig held it, waiting for her to move forward. But she was staring at Jake, her eyes cold and condemning.

Tess had said that Dora was on the committee. Jake remembered that much. He also remembered that Dora had called him irredeemable the day he told her he wasn't sorry that he had nailed Dirk Mulroon's nose when the boy had made comments about Jake's father. She had glared at him when he'd refused to answer her questions regarding the slander scribbled about her on the boys' bathroom wall. And he'd seen dark disappointment, maybe even hate in her eyes when she'd looked at him right after Cassie Pratt's sentence had been handed down. Somehow Jake didn't think Dora's opinion of him would change even if she knew the truth. They'd spent years in a cycle of defiance and punishment. Cassie had simply been a darker chapter of the same book.

Still, Jake's mother had taught him to be at least outwardly respectful. He gave Dora a curt nod. "Craig," he added, half expecting the man to flinch or to narrow his eyes.

Instead the robust man nodded back. "Jake," he answered in kind, then turned his attention to making sure the door didn't hit Dora as she struggled through.

Jake and Tess had taken several more steps when Jake heard Craig call his name. "Jake," the man repeated when he turned. "I guess I should…that is, I wanted to thank you for giving my nephew some of your time. My brother Ray won't take money from me, but I should have seen that all Paul needed was a little attention. I could have done that much at least."

Shrugging, Jake shook his head. "No need for thanks. Paul did his share of the work. I enjoyed the company."

Craig nodded then as he turned to go back in his store. "Okay, I'm glad, then. Really glad. Ray's my kid brother. He's had it rough."

The door closed behind him. *Ray Bickerson.* Jake tried to equate the somber man he'd met the other day when he'd escorted Paul home with his vague recollections of a pudgy little kid who had trailed Craig once. It was impossible. Too much time had passed.

He smiled down at Tess who was looking up at him.

"I'm sorry about Dora," she said, surprising him. "I think…she's an unhappy woman who's lived alone too long."

Worry was evident in her eyes and Jake couldn't help wanting to reassure her. It was, unfortunately, not a possibility.

"I'm sorry to hear that," he said, and he realized that it really was true. "But don't look to build any bridges between Dora and myself, Tess. We go back a long way. I was a defiant kid, and she made it clear I was not her kind of student the day I stepped into high school. We antagonized each other on a regular basis. So whatever happens tomorrow in that meeting happens, but don't think that just because Craig and I spoke to each other that the same thing will happen with Dora. It won't.''

She opened her mouth, then closed it again, biting down on the fullness of her lower lip in a way that was incredibly distracting. Jake was tempted to bend down and taste those ripe pink lips for himself.

Instead he cleared his throat and moved toward the park entrance and a nearby table.

"You could apologize to her," he heard Tess say, her voice just a touch above a whisper.

He turned to where she had moved up behind him, her hands clenching and unclenching, an anxious look on her face.

Jake couldn't keep from smiling even as he shook his head. "There's a word for people who say insincere things just to get their own way, sweet Tess," he reminded her. "Not a nice word, either. Besides, what would I tell her I was sorry for?"

A frown bunched Tess's brow. "I'm serious. And don't tell me you're not sorry for *anything* you did as a kid. Everyone in the world thinks back on all the stupid things they did in high school with some regrets. You could at least apologize for pinching Marilee Wilson's bottom.''

Jake looked down at her, unable to suppress a low, deep chuckle. "Who told you that, Marilee or Dora?"

A slight pink tinge had begun to creep up above the white of Tess's blouse. "Both, actually, although I don't think Marilee was complaining. When she heard you would be passing through, I almost think she considered presenting her fanny to you again, although I got the feeling that she was looking for a little more than just a pinch.''

The disgruntled sound of Tess's voice sent a bolt of pleasure coursing through Jake. He told himself that it was just the prissy schoolteacher part of her that was disgusted with the fact that he and Marilee had managed to disrupt a classroom. She wasn't jealous. There was no reason someone like Tess would ever be jealous of Marilee.

"I could apologize for that," he agreed. "It *was* a stupid thing to do. Anything else that I might genuinely regret that I could relay to Dora?''

He looked down into her eyes, she looked up into his.

"You could apologize for Cassie," she whispered.

The silence was enormous, it went on and on as the two of them stared at each other and the surrounding park seemed to disappear. She was waiting, she was hoping, really hoping Jake knew that she could absolve him of that sin. He wanted to say the words, but the honest truth was that he didn't regret that day with Cassie. She was a friend who had learned then that he would stand by her. He still had to do that. Not even for Tess could he try to save himself.

"Not for that," he answered, his voice low but firm. "I can't apologize for my relationship with Cassie."

Bitter disappointment was written in the dark violet of Tess's eyes, but she was a trouper. He had to give her that. She made a valiant effort to bounce back, taking a deep breath and giving a tight nod.

Tess stared up at Jake, trying not to think—or feel. She had felt so close to Jake just a second earlier. Now she had to face the fact that she would never really be able to understand this man, and in truth she shouldn't really be trying. He was just a client, one who would be on his way before the week was up.

"All right then, forget I said that," she said, forcing a false cheery note into her voice. "Let's look at those plans, Jake. What have you finally decided to do?"

He studied her for what seemed like long moments but was in fact only seconds. Jake was no fool. He knew that his denial had disappointed her, but he agreed to play along. He took her hand and led her to a nearby table.

"Here, see what your miracle contractor talked me into."

Carefully he unrolled the plans along with another sheet of paper covered in notes.

Tess studied the architectural plans. Some people might find the stark lines and figures boring, but she never did. "It's going to be lovely," she exclaimed, running her fingers over the smooth paper. "And, Jake, you're restoring the fireplace to its original form," she whispered. "You know you didn't have to do that. Masonry work is always expensive, and it wasn't required, especially when you don't even plan to stay around and enjoy it."

"*You'll* enjoy knowing that it's done," he said simply. "I remember how taken you were with that old photo in the scrapbook, the one where my grandparents were holding hands in front of the fireplace."

It had been a wonderful picture, a touching, romantic photo with Jake's grandfather staring lovingly down at the small woman beside him. His grandfather still had dark hair at that time, he looked a lot like Jake did now, and Tess was half afraid that *that* had been what she found so appealing about the picture.

He had remembered her comments, he'd been that

thoughtful. But then he'd always been thoughtful with her. Sometimes she looked at him and found it utterly unbelievable that he'd been a hellion. Then again, she sometimes looked into the startling green depths of his eyes, she felt the shiver run through her, and she knew that this man was capable of many unbelievable things.

Tess took a deep, shuddery breath. She tried to bring her attention back to the drawings, and she'd done so, *barely* done so, when she heard a couple quarreling and growing nearer.

"You stupid slut. All you're good for is having babies." The man's voice was slurred, harsh. A small woman struggled along, trying to keep up with his long strides as he gripped her by the arm.

"I'm—sorry, I didn't know you were saving that money. It was in the box where you keep the grocery money." She choked out the words and took another skip as he yanked her forward.

"Just shut up," he bellowed.

The woman closed her mouth, but a whimper escaped.

"Shut up," the thick-limbed man said again, dragging her like a doll. "When I get you home I'm gonna smack you good." His voice was filled with drunken promise. He was muscled and hairy and several times larger than the woman.

Tess stared openmouthed. She started to step forward, but Jake was already in motion. He placed his hand on her arm, stopping her momentum, then reached the man and woman in three quick strides. Without a word, he twisted, sliding his long body between the man and the woman.

"I'd let the lady go, Dirk," he recommended in a voice laced with granite and steel.

"Yeah? Well, who the hell do you think you are,

Walker? She's my wife.'' The man's voice was like thunder, his expression an ugly storm. He lashed out with one fist.

Jake easily sidestepped the clumsy punch, keeping the woman behind him.

"Then treat her like a wife, with some respect.'' Jake leaned into the man who leaned back slightly.

"Please,'' the woman whispered from behind Jake, her fingers grasping his arm to get his attention. "This will only make it worse.''

The man sneered. He took a step forward now. "She, at least, knows her place,'' he offered.

Jake's low laugh of derision was not pretty. "She knows you'll probably hit her for my interference, but you're not going to, are you?''

"I'll do what I want.''

"And so will I,'' Jake countered. "I always have. It would give me a lot of pleasure to flatten that nose of yours again, Dirk. And I will if I come visiting tomorrow and your lovely lady is damaged in any way. Only this time I won't stop with your nose. A broken nose is too light a sentence for a man who would assault a woman who can't possibly defend herself against a stronger force.''

"You aren't the first who tried to step into my business. That one there,'' he sneered, motioning to where Tess stood. "She called the cops in once, but she forgot that a wife has to press charges. Terry here ain't about to do that.''

Tess had kept her eyes on Jake. Fear for him rose within her, knowing as she did that Dirk was a man who'd have no qualms about fighting dirty. With Dirk's words dying away on a sneer, Jake turned to look at her. She could swear she saw concern and pride in his eyes, and...something else that she couldn't define, but she couldn't savor the thought or linger on it. She had to steer Jake's attention back to the man.

"I'm fine," she mouthed.

Jake swung around just in time to duck another clumsy punch.

"Well, Dirk, we won't have to worry about the law. I don't intend to call them in unless your wife wants their help," Jake assured him smoothly. "Don't touch her again, not in anger."

His words were final, filled with meaning. He stepped away and looked at the woman. "Is there anywhere you'd like to go? Anyone you'd like to stay with tonight?"

She looked at her husband, cautiously, fearfully. Long seconds ticked by. Then she gave a quick nod. "My sister lives two towns over," she offered. "She'll come get me if I call."

As she scurried away into a nearby store, her husband screaming oaths at her, Jake turned his back on Dirk as if the man wasn't even worth noticing now that his wife was out of sight. He moved toward Tess, even as she saw the anger building on the bull-faced man behind him. Dirk's meat-slabbed hands were shaking as he curled them into fists.

"Damn you, Walker. You were always trash. Your father was trash, and so are you."

Tess opened her mouth to warn Jake as Dirk charged, but she needn't have bothered. Jake stepped to the right. He twisted, and with one quick move threw Dirk to the ground. Standing over the man, he studied him as if he were an inconsequential insect that had wandered into town. Then he turned to Tess, holding out his hand as he moved away.

"I'm going to charge your hide with assault, Walker," Dirk sputtered, slamming his fists on the ground as he struggled to rise, then fell back again. "You'll go to jail for that, you know."

Jake didn't even turn. He didn't even acknowledge the man's words.

"Are you okay?" he asked Tess, folding her hand in his own and pulling her close to his side. "I'm sorry for that. Come on, let's go. I'll take you home and we can save these plans until tomorrow afternoon."

She wanted to talk, to tell him how grateful she was. Terry had lived such a hard life lately. But swift tears filled her eyes. She cupped her free hand over her mouth.

"Thank you," she finally whispered. "You're a good man, Jake."

She felt his fingers clench on her own. For a long time he didn't say anything at all. She wondered if he'd even understood her words, her voice had been so choked up.

"Don't think that," he warned her. "If you do, I'll be forced to tell you all the things I've done over the years, and I'd just as soon you didn't know."

But it was too late, Tess knew as she walked away. Jake might have sinned. The rumors that he'd once spent a night in jail for brawling might just possibly be true, and he probably *had* defied Dora every step of the way and said and done things he wasn't proud of. But he had not betrayed Cassie Pratt. She would not believe that. She just couldn't believe that any longer.

Jake Walker was a man who would never hurt a woman, not in the way people thought that he had. He would not abuse a woman or neglect a child. There was more going on here than people knew, a whole lot more than *she* knew or could even begin to figure out. No one, she'd bet, knew the real truth about Cassie and Jake except Cassie and Jake. And Jake wasn't talking.

That left Cassie.

And, Tess figured, it was well past time that the two of them met. Jake had done so much good here, not just for Terry and for Paul, but for herself, as well.

She wanted to give back a little if she could. Tomorrow she would finally go see Cassie Pratt and find out what Jake was really guilty of.

Chapter Nine

She wasn't coming. He wasn't going to see her today after all.

Jake hung up the phone, he tried not to think about the hesitant tone of Tess's voice when she'd explained that she would not be able to finish looking at the architectural drawings after all.

Something must have happened. She wanted to see those plans. This project meant a great deal to her. *Something* was wrong, and Jake knew just what it was.

She'd had time to think about that incident yesterday. Tess had finally seen him in his true skin. She'd seen how ugly and cold he could be. He'd wanted to step on Dirk yesterday. He'd really wanted to hit the guy when he'd seen how scared his wife had been, and there was no way he could have hidden that desire, especially not from a lady as perceptive as Tess. She would have seen just how deep his hatred of the man went, and civilized as she was, it would have shocked her, maybe even frightened her. It would have definitely made her think twice about spending time alone with a man whose emotions ran so close to the surface.

A hollow, empty feeling flooded Jake's soul. He was leaving tomorrow anyway. Tess's disgust of him shouldn't matter. He shouldn't care, he was never supposed to care. Hadn't he learned all too well that caring was painful and not for him?

What he needed now was a distraction. With a little work, he'd knock that feeling right out of his system. In just a short while he would forget that Tess even existed.

Picking up a sledgehammer, Jake headed for the upstairs bath and the ugly 1950's bathtub that needed to be broken up and removed. Hard, physical labor was what he needed to get the lady out of his mind. He had no doubt at all that a little exertion would be just the ticket. He'd be absolutely fine in just a short while.

Tess sat in her car outside the small cabin-style house anchored at the end of a dirt road. She'd made several wrong turns, but she was finally here. Now all she had to do was get her courage up and brace herself for what lay ahead when she hadn't a clue just what did lie ahead.

It had taken some time to locate Cassie's phone number. It had taken almost more guts than she had just to dial the number, and then she'd had to practically beg the lady for a face-to-face visit. Cassie had not wanted to meet with her, and after all, who could blame the woman given her past experience with Tess Buchanan?

Tess braced herself for the meeting. She realized that Cassie must know things about Jake—intimate things— that Tess herself would never know. What would it be like to listen to another woman discussing her relationship with Jake? What would she do if Cassie told her that Jake really *had* ruined her life?

Tess took a deep breath. She reached for the handle of the car, squeezing it so hard that the metal seemed to become a part of her hand.

She hated even admitting to those kinds of fears when she had been so absolutely certain of Jake's innocence just the day before. She didn't *want* to doubt him in any way, and Tess's heart lurched as she realized why she was so desperate to hear that he was innocent.

She cared for him. No, she cared for him too much.

Tess opened the car door. Maybe it would be smarter just to let all this drop. In a couple of months she would be married. It would be better if she didn't walk into her new life with any regrets about Jake.

She touched one toe to the ground.

She *wouldn't* have any regrets. Her match with Gray was sensible, desirable. It was the kind of marriage she'd learned was right for her. The fact that Jake's touch made her ache or that he invaded her thoughts way too often, couldn't have any bearing on her future. And right now she needed to think about the past, not the future.

Jake was innocent. She knew he was, and all she wanted was for Cassie to spell it out for her.

The slamming of the car door behind her as she left the refuge of the vehicle and made her way to the house punctuated her determination to separate the facts from the fiction.

She only hoped she could live with the results of to-day's conversation.

And then Tess had no more time for conjecture.

The door slid back and she was faced with a delicate, dark-haired woman with brilliant blue eyes. Knowing eyes, eyes that remembered…everything.

"Ms. Buchanan," the woman said, stepping back so that Tess could enter. Cassie's hair was braided, wrapped

around the crown of her head, giving her a regal look
that matched the cool eyes and the perfect posture.
"Come in. Sit down." She gestured toward a neat but
well-worn sofa where a small table was situated.

She waited until Tess was seated, then sat down in a
stiff-backed chair just opposite.

"You...have a very lovely home," Tess said, and she
meant what she said. The room was small but tidy.
Fresh-picked flowers in a simple but lovely vase scented
the air. The dark wooden floor was decorated with
bright, handmade rugs. Plain white curtains edged with
lace hung at the windows.

"Thank you," Cassie said, arching one delicate brow.
"Forgive me, Ms. Buchanan, but..." She held out her
hands in a gesture of surrender. "I don't think you came
here to discuss my decorating scheme. You and I haven't
met for eleven years, and I had the feeling that this was
a matter of some importance to you."

Tess felt swift color blossoming in her cheeks.
"You're right. Of course you're right, but I—"

"*You* are much more polite than I am," Cassie agreed
with a hint of laughter. "All right then, we'll pretend
for just a moment that you and I actually know each
other and this is purely a social call. Is Misunderstood
as pretty as ever in the summer?"

"In full bloom," Tess answered with a hesitant smile.
Her own reservations at getting right to the point *did*
seem silly now in the light of Cassie's straightforward
manner. Tess searched for the right words to ask her
questions, but—

"And are you and Gray Alexander still planning a
late fall wedding?" Cassie asked.

Tess jerked her head up. "You know Gray?"

Cassie shook her head quickly. "No. No, I don't *re-*

ally know him, but I read the regional papers. The two of you are in there quite frequently.''

''Yes, we're still getting married,'' Tess said firmly, ''but you were right before. I didn't come to make a social call. I came to talk to you about something more important.'' She took a deep breath, then stared Cassie full in the face. ''I've come to ask questions I should have asked a long time ago about things that are really none of my business, but—'' Tess held her hands out beseechingly. ''Jake Walker is back in Misunderstood temporarily. He and I have worked together. He's been...kind to me.'' Tess took a breath, she slipped her fingers around the edge of the chair. ''I've gotten to know him, to like him and, frankly...to doubt half of what I've heard about him.''

The other woman shook her head with a gentle smile. ''Only half?''

Tess blew out her breath. This was so uncomfortable. She was sure Cassie must feel the same. Invading the lady's privacy in this bold fashion really was unforgivable. Still, Tess pushed back that thought. She was determined to get what she came for.

''Jake is not a man to be taken lightly or one to underestimate,'' Tess conceded, ''but...are all the rumors true? Did he really get you pregnant and then leave you to deal with the consequences alone?''

The silence seemed almost like another person, an imposing person that took over the room completely for a moment.

Cassie looked up then, into Tess's eyes.

''Well, that certainly takes care of all that small talk, doesn't it? But...when you suggest that Jake might be Robbie's father, I'll remind you that *I* never said that.''

More silence as Tess digested that bit of information.

"You didn't deny it, either. Everyone thinks Jake has a child he's abandoned. Does he?"

Tess held her breath waiting for the other woman's answer. Cassis's eyes were filled with regret, Tess realized as the two of them studied each other.

"That bit of gossip has never surprised me, and yes, of course, I realize that the blame for that lies squarely at my door," Cassie acknowledged. "This is not something I discuss, Ms. Buchanan, not ever, but you're right in your assumptions about Jake. He is caring and special, and I can tell that you're concerned for him, so I'll tell you what I wouldn't tell you otherwise.

"That day, that spring, *I* was the one at fault. Jake and I had become friends. We had more than a few things in common. His father had been in prison, mine was a slave to alcohol. My family had no money, I wore hand-me-downs that never fit, and I always felt…different, but not with Jake. He never looked to see if my roots were showing, the way other people did. And I'm not telling you this in a bid for pity. Those days are past, but I just want you to know that Jake isn't all he's made out to be. When we were in school he was like a brother who looked out for me, and he's been good to me and my son for the past few years."

Tess looked into Cassie's eyes, eyes that demanded attention and understanding. "You've seen Jake lately?"

Cassie smiled slightly, returning Tess's gaze. "He's come here once since he's been in town. He tries to help me when I'll let him, but he's been pretty busy lately, I suspect."

Warmth flooded Tess's face. Cassie probably knew full well that Jake had been spending a great deal of his time with her and the house.

"I told you, Jake's…Jake's been a friend to me, too,"

Tess said, feeling an embarrassing need to explain her presence here when Cassie knew of her engagement.

The other woman tilted her head. "He's that way," she agreed. "Jake has a soft spot for women. But if you're wanting to know if Jake provides for me and Robbie, well, he tries to when he thinks I won't notice. I let him give Robbie gifts now and then, and he visits us when he can, but he does live in California, you know," the woman added. "Besides...there's really no reason for Jake to be responsible for us. Robbie isn't Jake's son."

Tess pressed her fingers against the floral pattern on the arm of the sofa. Soothing relief slipped through her. "It was difficult to believe he would desert you," she admitted, raising her chin so that she faced Cassie again. "He's been so considerate of me, but if he's not Robbie's father, then why haven't you—"

"Why haven't I told the world at least that truth?"

Still meeting the other woman's gaze, Tess nodded silently.

Cassie let out a sigh. She frowned, blowing out a breath. "It was...so long ago. I was different then, much more insecure. And I suppose at first I said nothing because I was ashamed that I had been caught in that closet with Jake, trying to do exactly what we were accused of doing. That day we were both expelled, I'd just realized I was pregnant and that the boy I worshiped would never want me or my child. I was young, scared, foolish, alone, and I needed someone to hold me and love me and make things right, to make me feel whole when I felt like I was falling to pieces. At that moment I wanted the only man I trusted to make me forget that I was alone in my misery. I turned to him the way I'd always turned to him."

Tess sucked in her breath, and Cassie shook her head.

"I only meant that I felt safe with Jake. That day, he knew I was upset about something, but I was the one who took the key to the closet, the one who pulled him down the hall by the hand. It was me who tried to make something happen that we both surely would have regretted later. I should have said as much at the time, but I was too ashamed and distraught, and I simply followed Jake's lead when the questions started coming. Rational thought flew out the window for a while. I was afraid that if I opened up and told the truth, I would spill everything."

"But Jake—"

Cassie nodded. "I know. Jake came to me before he left that night, upset because he thought he'd led me astray somehow. He told me his leaving was for the best. By then I'd realized that if I told him the truth, he would have offered to marry me. I let him go because I was afraid I might accept. A year later when he finally met Robbie, he did offer, but by then I was strong enough to say no."

Tess pushed a shaky hand through her hair, realizing how far this woman in front of her had come. From frightened child to strong woman, she'd been able to walk away from Jake's goodness and his concern when he'd offered to marry her and to protect her child. Tess wondered if she could have done the same. Could she have said no to a life with Jake? She closed her eyes, cut off the thought. Taking deep breaths to calm herself, she stared into Cassie's sad eyes.

"But you never did tell anyone Jake wasn't Robbie's father?" Tess said gently. Cassie's story called up her sympathies, but this was Jake they were talking about, and he had been condemned for a crime he hadn't committed.

"You're right, I didn't." Cassie held out her hands in surrender. "When I left and moved to a town seventy-five miles away, no one knew I was pregnant. It was easy to assume everyone would forget about Jake and me, and in truth, they almost did…until my pregnancy began to show. Then a little gossip reached me, but by then Jake was safely away, and people had taken pity on Flora and enfolded her in their arms. Bringing up old scandals when I had no intention of discussing Robbie's natural father seemed like something that would have just brought people running to stare at my son to see what man he looked like."

Cassie sighed. "Of course, today Robbie could probably deal with that. He's pretty confident and he knows my love for him is what's important," she said with obvious pride, "but back then he was so tiny, so vulnerable. I just couldn't risk exposing him to that, not even for Jake. Because really, who would have believed me? I had a baby out of wedlock. I broke into a school closet and tried to seduce a man. There would have been those who would believe I would also lie for Jake's sake, and to be honest, they would have been right…if it hadn't been for Robbie."

Cassie paused, crossing her arms over her chest. She shook her head when Tess opened her mouth to speak.

"One thing more. I want you to know that Jake has never denied Robbie and I don't believe he ever would. He knows as well as I do that a woman who made love to a man and was deserted would be offered sympathy, but a woman who slept with one man and was caught with another might well be an object of scorn. Jake didn't want people to know the truth. He didn't want anyone taunting Robbie with his mother's sins the way he was taunted as a child. Robbie and I have friends here, people who either don't know or don't care about my years in Misunderstood."

Tess nodded. She thought about all that Cassie had said, and she thanked all the stars in the sky that Jake was innocent of this at least. But the perception of guilt still existed—and there was a child at stake. The teacher in Tess stumbled forward. "I understand that, but—if Robbie thinks that Jake is his father, doesn't it hurt him to think he's been deserted? Wouldn't it be better for him to know that Jake visits because he cares, not that he stays away because he doesn't? Won't he learn the truth in time and want to know about his birth father?"

Cassie's chin firmed, grew more stubborn. A flicker of flame entered her eyes. "There would be no point in telling Robbie who his father was. Why offer him hope about a man who wouldn't want him? Robbie knows Jake isn't his dad, but he also knows Jake loves him. It's the best I can do."

Tess narrowed her own eyes.

"Except that Jake is back in town now, and the old rumors are flying again."

Cassie shook her head and smiled. "Jake said you were a very determined lady, but let me ask you this. If I tried to clear Jake's name now, would anyone other than you believe me after all this time? As I told you, my word doesn't mean much in Misunderstood. I'm a woman who broke the rules, and this is old gossip, fearfully entrenched and difficult to exterminate. It isn't the kind of thing a person can stand up and announce at a town meeting."

Tess leaned forward slightly. "You're right, it's not, even if I wish it were. But if someone asked you—"

"In that case, I would tell the truth. It's past time, and safe to do so now, but I doubt if anyone will ask."

Tess nodded. Cassie was probably right. No one had asked even when Cassie had turned up pregnant years ago, apparently. *Everyone* had assumed.

"Jake—" Tess began.

Cassie stood. She held out her hand. "My son will be home soon, Ms. Buchanan, and he'll be needing my attention, but please understand this. I love Jake as I've always loved him, and I promise you I'll do whatever I can to help make life easier for him. You'll have to take that on faith."

Tess blinked her eyes. Cassie was tall and proud, but she had obviously struggled to maintain that pride. She'd made mistakes and been condemned for them.

"We all do things we regret when we're young," Tess whispered. It was the second time she'd repeated that phrase. It was becoming her mantra, it seemed. "I made some mistakes myself," she confided. "Serious mistakes. You could have used another girl your age standing beside you that day, not sitting in judgment."

Cassie shrugged. She squeezed Tess's fingers consolingly. "As I said, I don't think any of us were thinking too clearly at the time. But I'm...glad that you came. I don't know if you can help Jake. He's big on giving help, but not much on accepting it himself. He can be just as stubborn as I am."

Tess couldn't help smiling at that. "I've learned, Cassie. I know that. And I agree that he wouldn't appreciate it if I stood up and announced his innocence to the world, but I'll do what little I can. And as for you...well, I hope you'll call me Tess from now on. Maybe we can get to know each other...as friends...when everything settles down."

Cassie smiled, but she gave a noncommittal shrug. "I don't visit Misunderstood."

Nodding, Tess walked through the door Cassie had opened.

"I don't go back to my hometown anymore, either. Perhaps we could meet here."

Cassie maintained her smile. "I appreciate that thought."

It was only after she had gone that Tess realized that Cassie had agreed to nothing approaching friendship. She couldn't really blame the woman, Tess thought, not when she herself was such a part of a painful past. But Cassie had at least agreed to help Jake if she could. She'd confirmed Tess's intuitions about him.

The man was living a lie and so was she. She was in love with Jake Walker, and just as Jake had done nothing about the gossip that surrounded him, so she would do nothing about her feelings for Jake. It wouldn't be fair to Gray—or to Jake. He'd already been the focus of one scandal. He didn't need a soon-to-be-mayor's wife throwing herself at him and throwing his life into undeserved turmoil again.

The cavernous room where the meeting was being held at the town hall was filled with premeeting chatter, but even looking down at the notes she'd scribbled to herself, Tess knew the minute that Jake walked in the door. She felt him even before the chitchat began to die down.

He was magnificent, tall in his black shirt and black slacks, his shoulders almost too wide for the doorway, and he was staring straight at her, smiling. She had to look away for fear he and everyone else in the room would see what she was feeling.

"Jake," Gray acknowledged, as the meeting got under way. "If you would just let us see the plans, I don't think this should take too long. I understand Tony drew them up, and he's more than qualified for this type of project."

Tess felt a moment of sadness that she couldn't feel the kind of heart-deep yearning for Gray as she did for Jake. He was a good man, a solid man, the best.

She would do her best to learn to love him. She swore she would.

Smiling his way, Tess steadfastly kept her eyes from Jake. She rose to look over the plans that she had seen only yesterday—a thousand years ago.

"Tony's good, all right, but he's not here, is he?" Dora asked. "I'd like to look at those a little closer, to make sure no changes have been made to the originals."

Tension coiled within Tess. She couldn't keep her eyes from Jake's then. He should have been staring at Dora, denying whatever petty accusation she was trying to make, but he was not. He was looking at *her,* at Tess. Calmly he held her gaze, he studied her expression, her furrowed brow...and then his face became a mask. Just like before, like the day he was expelled.

He wasn't going to answer Dora because...because he knew there was no point. Or maybe because he just didn't care about petty minds like hers.

But Tess cared. She shoved back from the table, clenching her hands into tight fists at her side. "What are you implying, Dora?" she asked, wondering at the coolness of her own voice.

The woman didn't hesitate. "He didn't want to do this in the first place, did he? Everyone knows that, so what's to stop him from changing the things he doesn't like? A little line here and there, we might not notice until it's too late.''

Tess fought her anger. She rolled her eyes heavenward. ''Don't insult his intelligence—or ours, Dora. We would know and so would Tony.''

''I didn't say Jake Walker was stupid. On the contrary, he's smart and devious. Sneaky. He got caught holding a cheat sheet to a test once in my class.''

Tess looked at Jake, and found that he was staring at her once again. She opened her mouth to speak and she could swear that he shook his head.

She ignored his warning.

''Jake wouldn't change the plans,'' she said slowly.

Dora snorted.

Tess took a deep breath. She felt a calming hand on her arm and turned to look at Gray.

''We'll look at the plans carefully,'' he assured Dora, and Tess couldn't keep herself from whirling on him even as she saw Jake rise to stop her.

''Jake wouldn't cheat,'' she repeated.

Gray looked at Jake and back to Tess. He blew out a breath and shrugged slightly. ''I'm not saying that he would or that he did, Tess,'' Gray said calmly. ''But we have to look at the plans carefully in any case.''

''I'm sure of Jake's integrity, and when Tony usually submits plans, we don't go over them with a magnifying glass.''

''Tess.'' Gray attempted to pull her away, but she would have none of it.

Gray threw out his hands in surrender. ''You're right, Dora was out of line. That's the gospel truth, Dora, and you're smart enough to know it. But I also think, Tess, that you might not be looking at this as objectively as you usually do. Jake would agree, I'm sure, that he's acted irresponsibly in the past. I'm sure he'd want us to double-check everything in order to give him a clean pass.''

She refused to look at Jake. She could almost feel him glowering at her, warning her to sit down and stop painting him up to be a saint. And the old Tess would have agreed. Gray's suggestion was insulting to Jake, but it made sense given the world as everyone knew it.

Only she knew the truth. She had known it for a while. Years ago she'd had the chance to make a difference and she had played it too safe. She'd let the opportunity go by. She'd always wanted safety and security and had never stepped over the lines. She was not black leather and motorcycles and jumping off of mountains. Nor had she ever wanted to be…until Jake. She'd never done impulsive things…until today when she'd sought out Cassie. Until right now when she was going to do what she'd told Cassie she'd be a fool to do.

This was the one thing she could do for Jake, the only thing she'd ever be able to give to him.

Placing her palms flat on the table, Tess stared straight into deep green eyes that held her gaze and refused to let go.

''Jake never acted irresponsibly toward a woman, if that's what you mean,'' she whispered.

''Tess.'' Jake's growl blended with Gray's strained drawl.

''I talked to Cassie just today,'' she continued, trying to ignore Jake as she faced the man beside her. ''She and Jake never had a child. The baby was another man's. She and Jake were friends and she just…went a little crazy with worry and pain and the need for comfort that day they were expelled. I can understand that. And I know that Jake didn't abandon Cassie. Someone else did.''

Tess leaned toward Jake. She wished that the room would melt away so that she could tell him she was sorry for not realizing sooner, but a sound at her side sent her turning toward Gray.

His eyes were closed, his skin was paler than the white walls.

"I'm—excuse me, please. I'm sorry," he managed to say just before he lurched slowly toward the door.

Tess moved toward him, but he waved her away. His hands were in fists, his gait was uneven.

As he cleared the doorway, a muffled thud could be heard, like something hitting the floor, like a man falling.

Jake turned to Tess. He studied her, his expression clearly concerned. "I'll make sure he gets home," he whispered for her ears alone, rising to his feet. And then he left the room, shutting the door on the silent group behind him.

Chapter Ten

"So you're the man that's been missing from the picture all these years," Jake said, walking over to where Gray leaned against the wall, one hand shoved back into his hair. "She never told me."

Gray looked up then, his eyes bleak and empty.

"Looks like you never knew, either," Jake conceded. He placed his own back against the wall and slid down to the floor, one knee bent, the other leg straight out in front of him. "I've always wondered who it was. I even asked her several times, demanded to know. She never would say, or rather, she said that it didn't matter."

Gray closed his eyes. He let out his breath on a shudder.

"I was...so sure it was you, Jake. Hell, I was so damned jealous. The cards all pointed to you. Cassandra...she and I only had one day together, one to-die-for day. And then for weeks after that she refused my calls, returned my letters. She'd said that she didn't think we should see each other any more or even write. Soon after that, they found her with you. I remember, I was away at college at the time. My father called to tell me the latest news about town. I was in such a rage, I wanted to put my fist through your face, but I had no right. I thought I had no right.''

''You didn't, not if she'd already broken things off with you.''

''She was carrying my child, she was alone. Or as good as alone, given her family.''

''And she chose not to tell you. She must have had good reason.''

''She had the baby alone,'' Gray repeated. ''I left her to see to everything herself. I've never even seen him.''

He shoved away from the wall, started for the door, then turned to Jake.

''I want to talk to her. You know where she lives.''

Jake stood, crossing his arms. ''I know. Of course, I know, but I'm not going to make it that easy for you. No way. She'll see you if and only if she wants to see you.''

Gray raised his chin. He opened his mouth, to protest, Jake assumed. Then he nodded slowly.

''I'll give you the chance to talk to her first, I won't barge in on her unasked. But—''

Jake tilted his head, waiting.

''But I want you to let her know that I'll want answers,'' Gray added. ''I would never have let her go through a pregnancy alone if I had thought the child was mine. I want Cassie to understand that I won't wait forever. I'll expect to talk, and I'll expect to meet my son.''

Shrugging his agreement, Jake watched as Gray slowly moved to the door. He'd want some answers himself now that he knew the truth, but he suspected that he already understood Cassie's motivations. Gray's family had been practically royalty in Misunderstood. He'd been groomed to rule all his life, not to raise babies, and his family, especially his father, would never in this lifetime have accepted a girl like Cassie, not even if Gray had actually loved her rather than simply lusted for her. She would have realized that. She would never have asked Gray for his help once she realized her situation.

Gray should have known that. He shouldn't have doubted her, but he had, and he obviously regretted his lack of faith. There was going to be hell to pay for this day. Tess had certainly opened an economy-size can of worms in her attempt to clear his own name.

Tess.

She was no fool. She would have put two and two together in those first few seconds. Of course she would have. She was engaged to Gray. What must she be going through now? What kind of hell was she facing?

Her world had flown apart in the space of seconds. She had to be hurting. She would need a shoulder...and he had some experience at that kind of thing.

He seemed to spend a lot of time comforting Gray's women.

Jake wondered how soon it would be before Tess and Gray began to piece their future back together again.

They would. It was clear that Gray wasn't the type to intentionally hurt a woman. He would always do the right thing in the end. And Tess, well, he knew from personal experience that Tess was the forgiving sort, the kind of woman who looked past people's flaws in a search for their strengths. She would get past this day. She and Gray would mend, they would wed.

But for now she would need...someone. Jake closed his eyes and steeled himself to see her in pain, knowing that the best he could do would be to offer her a hand to hold, arms to cling to.

The truth was that...he loved her, and he would do whatever it took to help her through this time, even encourage her to listen to Gray's side of the story. If marrying the man would make her happy, then he would do whatever he must to facilitate that wedding. Even if he died a thousand emotional deaths himself.

Taking a long, deep breath, Jake stepped back into the other room. Tess was sitting alone next to the window, her face turned toward the darkened pane.

As he moved to her side and fitted his palm to her shoulder, she turned. He felt the shudder slide through her, but she didn't raise her eyes to his as he expected. She didn't speak.

He'd been right. She knew. Of course she did, and the hurt went even deeper than he'd imagined. His Tess needed to be out of here, away from all this.

"Come on, sweetheart, I'll take you home," he said, folding her hand into his own. "Just let me—"

"No." Tess's voice was strained, but she stiffened as he touched her. She cleared her throat and rose to her feet.

"No. I'm...I'm fine," she insisted, still not looking at him. "Jake...thank you. I'm really all right," she added as if he couldn't tell that she was anything but all right, that it was going to be a long time before her world came together and she was *fine* again.

"Excuse me, everyone," she said, her voice surprisingly firm and determined. "But under the circumstances, I believe we should adjourn the meeting. We'll conclude this business at the first possible opportunity."

As the other members agreed, Tess grasped the back of the wooden chair and watched them file out until the room was empty of all but her and the man beside her. She knew she should look Jake full in the face and say something. She needed to reassure him and let him know that she really was handling the shock of the last few minutes. She was okay. But she couldn't do that, she really couldn't.

Her mind was a muddle of confusion, elation, and fear. The jolt she had felt when she'd first seen Gray's expression had melted away too quickly, replaced by...something she shouldn't even be thinking about.

Gray was an honorable man. He would want to do what was right, and he would need to be free to marry Cassie. She herself would be free to do exactly as she pleased and what would please her the most would be to...spend the rest of her life in Jake's embrace.

But— Tess finally looked up at Jake. She saw the concern in his eyes.

He had stepped to her side automatically. It was obvious he wanted to help her, but then hadn't Jake always been the unsung champion of distressed women? That need to comfort and protect was as much a part of him as his sexy green eyes. His hand at her back, the gentle tone of his voice meant...everything to her, but it really meant nothing. Jake was just being Jake, the most misunderstood man in Misunderstood. She was a woman in need and, of course, he would come to her rescue. That was all there was to it.

Tess sucked in a deep, hurtful breath.

Immediately Jake moved closer, ignoring her attempts to wave him away. "I'm taking you home, Tess," he insisted, stealing a hand around her waist.

The urge to lean into him, to soak up the warm male scent of him and push herself closer was almost overwhelming.

She stiffened her backbone and her shoulder. She stepped out of the circle of his arm.

"Jake, I'm really all right," she said firmly, determined not to let him do this to himself and to her this time. "Thank you for the offer, but I'd really like to be alone right now. I have to— Good night," she finished, unable to look at him any longer without launching herself straight into his arms. "Good night," she repeated in a strained whisper.

He didn't answer, but he stepped aside.

It was cold without him beside her, and it would be colder still lying in her summer-heated bed tonight thinking of all the years she would lie there alone without him.

She was happy, so happy that everyone finally knew that he was not such a sinner after all, but she was bright enough to know that her fading engagement wouldn't really make a difference in their relationship. That had been temporary right from the start, and their temporary time together was all but at an end.

She was leaving tonight because if she stayed with him, she'd be in his arms and maybe in his bed. He'd just divested himself of the responsibility for Cassie. There was no way on earth she wanted him to spend the rest of his life feeling responsible for Tess Buchanan.

She wanted him back in his own home, away from here. She did. Oh, yes, she did.

Tess exited the room, then turned as she heard Jake's nearly silent steps behind her.

He was only two feet away as she looked up to face him.

Jake arched a brow.

"Did you think I'd let you walk to your car in the dark?"

Tess closed her eyes, then opened them again as she felt herself swaying toward him, as though she couldn't keep her distance. Putting her hands out, she grabbed the door frame to keep her palms from seeking his chest.

He tilted his head, looking at her whitened knuckles.

"Jake, I don't want you to feel responsible for me. You're not to worry about me," she whispered fiercely, whirling to walk away.

"Like hell I'm not, Tess. Just try and stop me."

She would do just that. She really would, Tess thought as she finally drove off into the night with Jake's motorcycle close behind.

With Jake's mother gone and with Gray to worry about Cassie, Jake had no one to worry over.

She would be damned if she was the next needy woman Jake intended to take on. His days as the savior of emotionally bereft women were over, at least in this town.

And she would tell him so—just as soon as she could look him in the eye without needing to press her lips to his.

Jake felt as if hell had made an appearance in his brain the evening before. He'd been up all night. He'd heard Gray's car pull up across the street. Long after midnight, the angry red numbers on his alarm clock had told him. And he'd lain there in the dark, listening to his heart thudding slowly like a cumbersome kettledrum, as he tried not to imagine Gray offering Tess the comfort she had refused from his own lips earlier that night.

She loved the man. It was Gray's embraces she wanted, not his own, Jake had reasoned.

But now morning was here. He'd stumbled into town to be away from his urge to see her, and one of the first people he'd seen had been Craig. Leaning on his unused broom, an anxious look in his eyes.

"She all right?" Craig asked, as if he expected Jake to know.

"I...don't know," Jake admitted, caught off guard. Hell, he wished he knew. He ought to know. It had been cowardly not to check on her, even if she wanted him away. Even if he was afraid to trust himself in close quarters with her.

Craig's genuine concern loosened Jake's tongue. "She insisted she was fine last night when she left for home. But you know Tess."

The other man rubbed his chin. He stared at Jake hard. "You didn't hear?"

"I heard about Gray and Cassie," Jake assured him. He hated repeating gossip, but after last night, this wasn't gossip. It was fact, and with Dora present, it was probably already public knowledge.

He turned to go, but a silent touch on his arm sent him turning. Craig had his hand on his arm. A nonthreatening gesture, the man was shaking his head. "About Gray and Cassie," he agreed, "but I don't think we're talking about the same thing. Gray's packed his bags, he's booked a hotel outside of Hightower, and he's left town. At least temporarily. Barbara Parker, his secretary, told me so when she saw me in the diner just an hour ago."

A rush of hope, a thunder of rage, rushed through Jake. Gray had promised he'd wait until Jake talked to Cassie and he was sure the man meant it at the time. But...hell, would he himself have waited if he'd just found out that Tess had given birth to his son many years ago?

Jake shook his head, knowing he would never have been able to stay away.

"What about Tess? Are she and Gray—?"

"The engagement's off," Craig confirmed.

Jake wanted to know more. A hundred questions clattered about in his brain. *Where was she now? Home? Had she left when he hadn't been looking? If she wouldn't take his help, was there someone else she could talk to?* Did she have any family left to turn to? But the best place to find those answers was from Tess herself.

He turned to go, stopping only long enough to give Craig a curt nod. "Thanks for telling me," he said, striding toward his cycle.

"Take care of her, Jake. I'm worried about her," the other man admitted.

Jake stopped. He and Craig stood studying each other, and he knew in that moment that Craig loved Tess, too, in his own way. She was that kind of woman. The whole town was probably worrying about her.

"If I have to, I'll drag him back here," Jake said. "He may think his responsibility lies with Cassie, but I know that woman. She's ten kinds of independent, and she isn't going to want to share her son with a man who's been gone for eleven years. If Tess wants him back, I'll do my best to convince the man."

But right now, Jake thought, roaring off down the street, the question was how to convince himself to keep from feeling relief that Tess's wedding was off. He had no business being glad that Gray was gone when the man's defection meant heartache for Tess.

And right now, he thought, striding up to her door and ringing the bell, what he needed to think about was how to comfort Tess without touching her.

And then she was there, opening the door, looking up

at him, and Jake gave up on thought. He just opened his arms and pulled her into them.

Her cheek was against his chest. She was sweet and soft and for several seconds she seemed to lean into him. She lifted her arms as if to wrap them around his waist.

And then she went still. She stepped away.

The old, familiar pain cut a path through Jake. She didn't want him to touch her. Automatically he fixed his facial muscles into the mask he'd perfected over the years. He began the process of burying his emotions.

But then Tess looked up at him, her eyes deep plum against her too-pale skin. He read the uncertainty in her eyes, and his heart wouldn't listen to his head.

"You heard," she said simply.

To hell with his own feelings. Tess was all that was important. "I'm so damn sorry, angel," was all he said, and he held out his open arms again.

Tess closed her eyes. He was sorry. Of course he was sorry, but for a few brief seconds there when he'd first shown up, she'd felt like she'd come home to the haven of his arms. As much as she respected and cared for Gray, her broken engagement had been right. It had felt right. And being up against Jake's heart had felt more than right. Free for the first time to touch him without guilt, she had felt…whole.

But *he* had been feeling pity.

She'd known it was coming. She'd even thought she'd prepared herself for it, but…

Tess looked at Jake's hands as he waited for her to take his body and use it. He would wrap himself around her and offer her comfort, but comfort was not what she wanted from him. She wanted…Jake, finally Jake. She wanted to be free to touch him in all the ways a man and a woman touched. She wanted to be able to love him, but that was not what he was offering.

Tempted to grasp what she could get anyway, Tess took another step away. She tipped her chin up, firmed her resolve and stared him in the eye.

"There's no need to be sorry, Jake. My breakup with Gray was amicable. We couldn't have stayed engaged given the circumstances."

"The circumstances being that Gray fathered Cassie's son?"

It was the first time the words had actually been spoken between them. Perhaps it should have hurt, but it didn't. Mostly Tess still found it hard to believe. Gray had never been impulsive or particularly passionate.

"Yes," she agreed calmly, "and because Gray's responsibility *does* lie with the two of them more than me. But also because Gray and I didn't have a conventional relationship, anyway. We didn't…love, not the way a husband and wife should love."

Jake stared long and hard into her eyes. He slid his palms up to cup her face. She swallowed hard and turned her head to the side, touching her lips to his skin. It was the closest she could get to telling him how she felt without actually saying the words.

"I'm not sorry I told everyone that you were innocent, Jake. And I'm not pining away over Gray." She lifted her face to his then, willing him to understand what she was saying.

Breath to breath, they stood there, and it was all she could do to keep from begging him to kiss her. His lips were that close, her need was that great.

"Tess." Jake's voice was strangled and thick. "Don't look at me like that. You need safety, security. I know you. You told me about how irresponsible your father and your husband were. I don't want to hurt you by bringing this up, but those things are important to you, Tess. I want you to have them. Right now you're feeling disoriented, adrift, and I'm here for you. I'm not going until your world is back together again.''

She closed her eyes and his words loomed larger, echoing after his voice had died down. He was worrying about her, but he hadn't said a word that sounded like he wanted her for his own, not in a permanent sense.

Need lanced through Tess. Frustration cut her to the quick, calling forth a boldness that she would once have been incapable of. She placed her palms on Jake's shoulders. She pushed herself high against him until she could whisper near his ear.

''I am not even slightly heartbroken about Gray, Jake Walker, but I am getting darn tired of you treating me like I'm some breakable bit of china. While I appreciate the kind thoughts, pity is the last thing I want from you.''

Jake felt her voice slip through him, warm puffs of her breath against his ear. She was up against him, her soft breasts crushed to his chest, her fingers twining about his neck. Hip to hip, with only the minor details of clothing separating his skin from hers, sanity began to subside. Slowly, slowly. What had she said? She didn't want his pity.

He knew that feeling, and hell, he had never wanted pity, either. What he wanted right now was far from pity. What he wanted—no, what he had to have—was Tess. Immediately. Pressed even closer. His mouth on hers, his hands sliding over her skin, his soul sneaking slyly into her keeping.

''If you think pity is even close to what I feel for you, then let me rectify your mistake, Tess.''

Jake brought one big hand up against her back, tugging her closer into the lee of his thighs. He cupped her head with his other hand, meshing his fingers in her hair.

"This is what I'm feeling Tess," he managed to say as she looked up at him, her eyes wide and soft and full of want. She was heaven in his arms. She was Tess, and when she tilted her face higher, he couldn't have stopped himself from claiming her lips if an entire crew of squad cars had shown up and threatened to lock him away for life if he touched her.

For long moments, paradise opened its doors. Tess snuggled close to him. She tightened her grip. Her mouth moved beneath his own, opening for him to taste. She pressed herself closer.

She was his. The thought settled in his mind like soothing, fulfilling water after a long, hot day. She was his.

She was his—for now.

"Jake," she said on a sigh as he pulled his lips from hers and gazed down at her. Adoration was written in her eyes.

"You fascinated me from the first," she said simply. "I always knew you were special."

And he knew this was just a fantasy moment in time. She was his—for now, but not forever. He would not let her get hurt again.

Tess reached up to kiss him again, but he cuffed his hands around her wrists. He gently pushed himself away from her.

"Don't," he said simply. "I know what you're thinking. I didn't impregnate Cassie, and no, I didn't do that, but I allowed her to break into an off-limits area at school when I could tell she wasn't thinking clearly. I went along with her seduction scene in an effort to help her in some stupid kid way when I should have simply demanded the truth from her. What's more, sweet Tess, thank you for defending me to Dora, but I *did* have a cheat sheet for that test. I had a chip the size of a mountain on my shoulder and because Dora knocked it off now and then, I did everything I could to make her life hell. What's more—''

Tess rose on tiptoes. She pressed her hand to Jake's lips.

''I'm sure you did many things you're sorry for now, Jake. I've had my share of experience with kids who have chips on their shoulders. With the proper supervision, they usually grow up to be fine adults, and I can see that your mother gave you very proper supervision. You're a warm, caring man who happened to be a pain in the neck as a child.''

Smiling up at him, Tess removed her fingers from his mouth and dropped a soft, warm kiss on his lips.

Jake couldn't stifle his groan even as he set her firmly away from him. ''Tess...'' he drawled. ''My father was an ex-con who killed himself driving drunk head-on into a tree three weeks after he got out of jail. I was a kid with an attitude, and I was far worse than a pain in the neck. If it hadn't been for Cassie and my mother and a few good teachers, I'd probably be my old man's clone.''

She opened her mouth to protest, but Jake's eyebrows drew together. He stopped her with a frown.

''I want you, Tess. So much I can barely even breathe. But it's not enough. Passion—even love isn't enough if I can't offer you the kind of future you deserve. You've built a home here where people revere and respect you. I don't want people whispering about you behind your back. Ever. It's not enough to care for you if I can't erase my past—and I'm not sure that I can.''

Tess placed gentle hands on his arms. She rose on tiptoe to look into his eyes. ''Now that people know about Cassie...''

Jake looked down into her hopeful, wistful, beautiful eyes. He drew his hand gently down the side of her face, stroked his thumb across her lips.

''It's not enough, Tess,'' he said, brushing a kiss over her forehead. ''Not nearly enough.''

Before he could go any farther, before he could kiss her lips or allow himself to even consider staying longer and trying to tie her more tightly to him, Jake stepped back. He turned and made his way away from her, wondering if he would ever allow himself to be this near to her again.

Chapter Eleven

For the first time since she'd moved to Misunderstood, Tess's house seemed like a prison. Her small, cozy bed was way too big, the rooms felt too empty, the floors sounded creaky and lonely. And the possibility that she would spend all her years alone here while Jake moved on and away kept her wide-eyed and weary, unable to sleep.

In fact, she wanted to step outside her skin and scream, to call him up and insist that he didn't have to prove himself to her. If he knew her, well then, she knew him, too. It didn't matter what his father had done, it didn't matter that he'd been a troubled and troublesome young man. She knew him and what she knew was that he was good and kind. She loved him with a love greater than any she'd ever known, and he didn't have to erase anything about himself. She didn't want him to erase a thing.

But, Tess thought, rising from her tousled bed and pulling on her robe, she could say all that and it wouldn't matter. Jake would not let her love him if he couldn't change his reputation in this town. Even if he never saw Misunderstood again, even if she didn't need him to do this, he would do his darnedest to turn the past upside down. He would sacrifice for her the way he'd left the town in sacrifice for Flora Walker. And if he didn't succeed...if he didn't succeed, then what?

He would leave her alone. That's what he would do. He would darn well never come near her again.

And how in the world could Jake change the past? People's memories were what they were, imprinted, a part of the mind like the scent of bacon frying or the color of leaves in the fall. Memories, rounded by the senses, colored by repetition and the passing of years. Like an ever-present videotape, they could be replayed over and over, their grainy patterns unchanging and always...there. So what could Jake do? Nothing. And if he could do nothing, then...

Tess blew out an angry breath. She would not sit here waiting for her fate and her love to be decided with no input of her own. She was a woman of action, and if Jake needed for his slate to be wiped clean, then she would be a part of that. Years ago she had stood aside and watched while his future seeped away. But she was not that girl anymore. She was no longer the woman who always opted for the safest, most secure route. Fate and time and her feelings for Jake had seen to that.

Picking up the phone, Tess began to dial.

In a matter of minutes, she had Dora on the phone. No point in putting off unpleasant encounters. Tess tangled the cord around her fingers again and again as she waited.

"Hello? Who is this?" Dora's voice came over the line, harsh and snippy.

"It's Tess, Dora. I'm just calling to begin the voting procedure on Jake's renovation plans. Did you look at them carefully?"

Tess herself had done so. She knew there was absolutely nothing wrong with the plans.

The only answer to her question, however, was some rather huffy breathing on the other end of the line.

"Dora?"

"I'm here. I looked, and I'm still thinking. There could be problems."

Tess passed a weary hand over her eyes. "There are no problems, Dora," she managed to say in a somewhat calm voice. "You've seen plenty of these things. Everything was in order."

"That's not what I mean."

"Just what do you mean?" Tess couldn't keep the edge from her voice.

There was a pause at the other end of the line. "Do we really want a man like that living in our midst? What if, when everything's finished, he decides to stay?"

The venom in Dora's voice was unmistakable. Her words sizzled and popped.

Tess closed her eyes. If he would only stay...but she knew that the house had little to do with his plans, and she couldn't ignore the very real anger that Dora was transmitting.

"That's...always been a possibility, Dora. You knew that right from the start, and that's really not the committee's concern."

The pause on the line was so long that Tess almost thought the other woman had hung up.

"Dora?"

"I never thought he'd really show his face again. Not after eleven years."

"This is his hometown. That's his mother's house."

"But…"

"But why are you so set against him, Dora?"

More silence, more huffy breathing. "The first day he walked into my class, it started. He crossed me at every turn. If I said sit, he stood. If I said no, he said yes. Not with words. No, he never argued. He just did as he pleased, just looked at me, ignored me. I sent him to the office, over and over. But he was a smart kid and his mother begged the school to let him stay. So he stayed, always staring me down with those insolent eyes of his. He thwarted me again and again, and made me look bad as a teacher."

"I'm sure it was frustrating, Dora, just as I'm sure he had a difficult time after his father went to jail. He was a hurt and angry child then, and he's a grown man now."

"I don't like him."

"That's not the point."

"You can't make me vote the way you want me to."

Tess counted to ten, she squeezed the receiver.

"Dora, this isn't a matter of voting your feelings. There's no reason not to accept those plans, and I'm sure you'd find it impossible to come up with a logical reason why we should turn them down."

A tapping sounded in Tess's ear, as if Dora was trying her darnedest to come up with a good argument.

"Then there was no real reason to call me, was there?"

"It's a technicality, Dora. Nothing more. In order for me to give Jake the go-ahead, I need a vote."

"Then I guess there's no more to say. I guess I'll have to vote to accept the plans."

But it was starry-sky clear from the sound of her voice

and her words that she would never accept the man behind the plans.

Tess sighed. She wondered who else Jake had crossed horns with in town when he was growing up. She wondered what it was like to grow up having people look at you and wonder if you would someday become a criminal like your father. Even in this modern day, people still tended to look for the father's bad habits recreated in the son.

Still, when she called the other members of the committee—all except Gray who'd given the thumbs-up to the plans before he left town—there was no problem. Tony's drawings were, after all, perfectly acceptable. Jake had the committee's blessing.

The town would give him a permit with no problem. Work could begin right away. Jake could wash his hands of this house and move on if he wished.

Wandering through the still, silent house, Tess thought of what Jake had said, that he couldn't love her if he couldn't erase the past.

Dora's ugly words played in a repeating loop running through Tess's mind.

People remembered what they wanted to remember. What if everything they remembered about Jake was bad?

What if he never let her close enough to tell him that she loved all of him, all he was now and all he'd ever been?

The revving engine of a motorcycle brought her spinning out of her worries and rushing to the window just in time to see Jake riding his cycle away from his house.

What if he left town again without telling her and never came back?

* * *

"Please leave a message." Jake's scratchy voice clicked off, followed by a beep and then a long stretch of silence.

Wild panic swept through Tess's body. Every time she'd called Jake, she'd gotten the machine, but not Jake in person. Never Jake.

Five times she'd started to cross the street to his house. Five times she'd stopped herself.

He wouldn't want her to come. He had his reasons.

Dumb reasons, her heart cried. Meaningless reasons. But not so dumb to Jake, and certainly not meaningless to him or to plenty of other people, Tess thought, remembering Dora and recalling Gray's attitude toward the man.

But two days had passed. Maybe he'd changed his mind, maybe if she stood up in the center of town and told the world that she loved him and she didn't care what he'd done years ago, he'd come to her.

But she knew he wouldn't. He just wouldn't.

Still, she would do anything for the chance to draw him near to her again. He'd been holed up in his house for two days—or maybe he'd gone.

Tess looked out the window again. Was Jake's bike behind the house...or was it gone? Was he gone?

Her heart beginning to thud hard against her chest, she opened the door and stepped out onto the porch. She would just go over there and look. She would just make sure he hadn't left her behind.

Craning her neck, she peeked around the side of the house as she moved. She crossed to the center of the road and listened for a sound.

And she heard it, a faint tapping from inside. She saw the rear wheel of his bike behind the lilacs.

He was there. He knew she was here.

He just hadn't come, and he hadn't called either. Maybe he'd changed his mind about caring. Maybe he was just going to pack and go soon.

Turning slowly, Tess retraced her steps. She picked up the morning paper she'd kicked aside, letting it sag low from her fingertips as she walked inside.

The paper slipped out of the clear plastic bag it was encased in. She'd been holding it upside down and the slight whoosh as it fell to the floor made her turn and look. She automatically bent to pick the pages up off the floor.

Jake's image stared back at her. A younger Jake, a yearbook picture no doubt.

The story was simple. Jake had been given a permit to restore the house. Work would start immediately. The house would be a great addition to the neighborhood. The owner was considering selling the property once the restoration was completed.

Tess brushed her hand across her lips, swallowing the pain that sluiced through her. He *would* be leaving. He wasn't going to come to her. Maybe he thought she would throw herself into his arms again, and he was trying to avoid letting her down easy.

The paper sagged in her hand, the top side flipping back, the bottom jutting upward. A small boxed blurb stood out in the lower right-hand corner.

"It was I, Emil Lattimore, not Jake Walker, who robbed Martin's Dimestore of two dollars and ten cents in July of nineteen seventy-eight."

Tess pulled the page closer. She let her eyes rove over the rest of the page.

It was I, Randy Dison, not Jake Walker, who started the fire in the art room sink in Mrs. Pierpont's room in nineteen seventy-six..."

"I, George Alden, confess that it was I, not Jake Walker, who wrote all the gossip about Ms. Averly on the boys' bathroom walls at the high school. I also stuck an ice pick into Mr. Richardson's tires and let Jake take the blame for it."

Confessions.

A fragile bubble of expectation began to grow in Tess. It expanded, filling her chest, making it difficult to breathe normally or even to think. Still clenching the paper, she turned and slammed out through the door, letting the screen door fall shut in a clattering bounce.

Her hair lifted off her neck as she hurried down the steps and practically flew across the road to Jake's house.

She didn't hesitate, she didn't knock, she didn't wait.

Planting both hands on his door, Tess gave a push and stumbled inside.

He was standing with his back to her, his broad shoulders filling her line of vision, her senses. He held a claw-hammer as he pulled nails that had once hung paintings and shelves on the west wall. But with the noise of the still-rocking door, the scrabble of her shoes on the warped wood, he turned slowly. He stared at her with dark green eyes that waited.

She wanted to move close, but she wouldn't let herself. Not yet. "Jake, what's going on?" she demanded suddenly in a hushed yet urgent voice.

He stood looking at her as if he could just gaze his fill forever, as if she hadn't just asked him a question.

"I've decided to stay and work on the house," he said

simply, but his low, strained voice was like a gift. Tess realized she'd been half afraid she'd never hear him speak to her again. But here he was. Not moving. Not...packing.

A small bit of eagerness rose within her. Tess tried to push it back. "That's not what I meant," she whispered. "Jake, why is everyone in town suddenly so eager to confess old sins?" She held out the paper. "Don't you think this will only make things worse? Won't everyone think you held a gun to these people's heads?"

She closed her eyes, willing herself not to hope too much.

Jake looked at her and felt himself tremble with the need to touch her, just to step one inch nearer to her. These last few days had been hell, trying to find enough jobs to keep his hands and mind away from her. He'd all but died trying to stay on his own side of the street. Every time the phone had rung, he'd fought the urge to pick it up to see if she was on the other end. And he knew she had been. There'd been too many hang-ups with no message at all.

But he'd had to wait. It had been all he could do. If things hadn't worked out...he still didn't know if things really could work out.

"Tess," he whispered, tossing down the hammer and moving close enough to catch the sunny woman's scent of her.

"Won't they think the worst of you?" she asked.

"And do you really think I would ever think less of you if they did?"

He shook his head. "They won't think I forced those confessions," he said, "because the people who wrote them know that I didn't threaten."

"So how did you—"

Jake smiled then, slightly, for the first time in days. "I took a page from your book, sweet Tess. I reasoned that time and the people we grow to love, might make a difference not just in my life, but in other people's lives, too. All these names..." He slid his palm beneath her hand that held the paper, lifting it up to kiss the fragile skin of her fingers. "Those people were all scared little kids years ago, and they acted the way scared little kids sometimes do, letting others take the blame. With my spit-in-your-eye disposition, I was an easy choice for a scapegoat. But those kids grew up, and for some, their guilt had been preying on their minds for years. They wanted to spill their guts and had for some time."

Tess let the paper slip from her fingers. She looked straight up into his eyes and smoothed her hand along the line of his jaw. "So why now?" she asked.

Jake brought his hands to her waist, holding her close, but not so close that she couldn't step away if she wanted to. "Because I asked them to," he said simply. "Because for the first time in years I went to another human being and asked for something for myself."

Her face was tilted up to his, so he saw the tears form in her violet eyes as she stood there, shaking her head. "Because you wanted to clear your name for my sake. Jake," she whispered. "You didn't have to do that, to humble yourself like that. Not for me. I don't need a hero—or a saint. And don't tell me you're neither of those. I know some of what happened in your younger days, and I know for certain you didn't lead an exemplary childhood, but you're...you're the best man I've ever known."

One tear had slipped down her cheek and Jake thumbed it away. He smiled into her eyes. "I *am* no hero," he admitted, ignoring her instructions. "Because

I did do my share of raising hell. More than I'll probably ever feel comfortable having you hear about. And there will be some people who'll never forgive me for what I was and whose son I am. My father was liked by plenty of people before he robbed that store. That kind of thing makes people wary. There may be some who'll never trust me, Tess."

"Like Dora?" Tess leaned back in his arms.

He followed her there, tilting his head to kiss the side of her neck. "Definitely Dora," he murmured against the delicate skin against his lips. When he lifted his head, he couldn't help the frown. Was he being fair to her? Could he take what she was offering?

He met Tess's violet gaze, noted the firmness of her lips.

She crossed her arms against his chest. "I don't need a superhero, Jake." She raised both eyebrows in that imperious way she had. "I don't even want one."

"No?" He raised one of his own lazy eyebrows. "What then?"

She smiled up at him, then closed her eyes.

"I'm not sure I can look at you when I say this."

Jake frowned with confusion.

"Tess?" He dragged her closer, fitted her to him. He would have stitched her body to his if he could, he was that unsure of what he was doing. He could still leave her, and maybe for her sake, that was just what he should be doing.

"Jake, I want—" Her voice came out in a choked whisper. She cleared her throat and tried again. "What I want is your hand up *my* dress," she said. "All these years, I've been jealous of Cassie. All this time, some-where, somewhere where I wouldn't even let myself think of it, I've been wishing that it was me in that closet with you.''

Relief, the certainty that he was right for this woman and she was right for him, gushed through him like healing water. A long, low chuckle escaped Jake's lips and he pulled Tess closer into the circle of his arms. ''Tess, love, I didn't really have my hand up her dress,'' he drawled. ''She was my friend, and she was hurt and frantic, a whirlwind of motion and need, and things just got a little crazy. I was trying to calm her, and it's possible that in my clumsy efforts to hold her still and get her to talk to me, I might have grabbed her. Her dress might have pulled up a bit. My hand must have been somewhere about here.'' He reached down, palming the back of her leg just above her knee.

Instant heat slammed through him. He sucked in his breath.

Tess took a deep, shuddery breath and managed a weak smile. ''It's different this time, isn't it, Jake?'' She clutched the lapels of his shirt and pressed herself closer. ''You don't even have to touch me. Just being near you makes me vibrate with need and want.''

Jake slid his hands behind her back, snugging her high against his chest. ''I'm desperate to be your lover,'' he admitted. ''But I want more than just your bed and your sweet body, Tess. I love you, angel, and I want your love in return. I want us to have the kind of love that a man and woman should share.''

His words slid into Tess's heart and soothed the ache that she'd been holding inside for days, for weeks. Slipping her fingers into his hair the way she'd always wanted to, Tess raised her lips to his and dropped a soft kiss there.

''You already have my love, Jake, all of it. I loved

you even before I spoke to Cassie. My heart knew the truth about you even then.''

"Did your heart know that mine stopped beating every time I thought of you married to someone else?''

Tess shook her head. "No, but I don't think I could have married Gray in the end, no matter what had or hadn't happened. Knowing that what I felt for you was what I should be feeling for my husband, it would have been wrong to go through with the wedding.''

"I couldn't have stayed and watched if you had.''

"And I couldn't have stayed if you'd gone.''

Smiling down at the woman he loved more than life, Jake lowered his mouth and claimed her for his own.

"I want you to have all the happiness there is. I want you to have a world filled with butterflies. You're too good for me, you know,'' he said, trailing kisses along her jaw.

Tess turned her head. She caught his mouth, then ended the kiss with a smile. "You're wrong,'' she said. "So very wrong, because together we're so very good.''

And when she brought her lips back to his, Jake knew that she was right. Together they were absolutely perfect.

The next morning Tess sat across from Jake at the Silver Platter Diner. He put his cup of coffee down and reached out to cover her hand in a possessive gesture that he would never have made a few days earlier.

Tess turned her hand over within his light grasp and twined her fingers with his. "The town is practically vibrating with the news about Gray. I have to admit that I find it hard to believe myself.''

Jake stroked his thumb across her wrist. "That he dropped out of the mayoral race or that he's camped out on Cassie's property line in a leaky old trailer?''

Shrugging, Tess concentrated on the joy of feeling free just to hold hands with the man she loved. "Both, I guess. Do you think they'll be able to work it out?"

Jake's fingers clenched over her own. "No, Cassie's changed. On the other hand, Robbie *is* his son. She can't deny that." Jake stilled his movements and looked into Tess's eyes. "Hell, I don't know, angel. Maybe they'll be able to patch things up, but there's a lot of years and tears there. Who can tell what's going to happen?"

Tess nodded. She cupped her hand around a few grains of spilled sugar on the table and concentrated on moving them into a small pile. "And what about us, Jake? Will we be moving back to California?"

Jake released her suddenly, stilling her movements. He reached out and put one finger under her chin, tipping her head up. "No. You love this town, it's a part of who you are, and…even if you don't need a hero, I need to do this for you. And for me, too. I want you to teach me how to love Misunderstood again, Tess. You're the woman who can do that, you know."

She took his hand in her own, rubbed her cheek against it. "You don't have to do this for me, Jake."

"I know. But let's do it for us. Let's move into that big house once it's done and raise enough kids to fill the place. I'll work on my image so they can be proud of their dad."

The love that filled Tess's soul in that moment could not be contained. One solitary tear leaked from beneath her lid and slipped down her cheek. "I love you, Jake Walker. Every single part of you, everything I know and have heard about. I love…you and only you."

Jake splayed his hand beneath her hair, resting his fingers against her scalp. There was a table between them, a world of people surrounding them.

"Would you mind very much then, Tess, if I kissed you right this moment, here, in front of everyone?"

Tess smiled. She slipped out of her seat and went to stand by his side. "I've been waiting to kiss you for eleven years, Jake. Try and make me wait a moment more."

And as he rose to his feet, Tess raised herself on her toes and pressed her lips to his. She twined herself close and opened her mouth, inviting him inside.

Jake was lost in her sweet depths. The diner melted away, the noise faded away to a joyous rushing of wind, and the only thing that mattered was the taste of Tess, the feel of her.

The sound of a waitress dropping a tray filled with glasses finally snagged his attention, and Jake raised his head. He looked down into Tess's loving eyes. Two tables away he noticed Craig Bickerson smiling at them while he ate his bacon and eggs. The Reverend Harper raised his coffee cup in a toast.

In full view of the morning crowd, Tess slipped her arms around Jake's neck. "It was worth every minute of the wait," she whispered. "We should definitely do that more often. Maybe in the middle of the town square, on the hammock in my yard, or…I know the locations of a few dozen closets that are available. It really doesn't matter where. Just kiss me again, Jake."

And she smiled up at him. She stood on her tiptoes and pressed her lips to his…until the world began to spin and whirl, until nothing else mattered except the lady in his arms and the promise in her eyes.

"Tess, you're such a wicked woman," he murmured against her mouth.

He felt her lips turn up in a smile against his skin.

"That's all right," she whispered. "My husband-to-be likes me that way."

"*Loves* you," he corrected, taking her hand as he tossed money down on the table and led her past the morning crowds. "I love you and all that you are. Completely."

And he kissed her once more as the morning breakfast crowd broke into a strong, steady round of applause.

* * * * *

**Share in the joy of yuletide romance with brand-new
stories by two of the genre's most beloved writers**

DIANA PALMER

and

JOAN JOHNSTON

in

LONE STAR CHRISTMAS

Diana Palmer and Joan Johnston share their favorite
Christmas anecdotes and personal stories in this
special hardbound edition.

Diana Palmer delivers an irresistible spin-off of her
LONG, TALL TEXANS series and Joan Johnston crafts an
unforgettable new chapter to **HAWK'S WAY** in this wonderful
keepsake edition celebrating the holiday season. So
perfect for gift giving, you'll want one for yourself...and
one to give to a special friend!

Available in November at your favorite retail outlet!

Only from

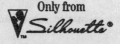

Look us up on-line at: http://www.romance.net   JJDPXMAS

SHARON SALA

Continues the twelve-book
series—36 HOURS—
in October 1997
with Book Four

FOR HER EYES ONLY

The storm was over. The mayor was dead. Jessica Hanson
had an aching head...and sinister visions of murder.
And only one man was willing to take her seriously—
Detective Stone Richardson. He knew that unlocking
Jessica's secrets would put him in danger, but the rugged
cop had never expected to fall for her, too. Danger he could
handle. But love...?

For Stone and Jessica and *all* the residents of Grand Springs,
Colorado, the storm-induced blackout was just the beginning
of 36 Hours that changed *everything!* You won't want to miss a
single book.

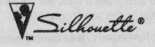

Look us up on-line at: http://www.romance.net   36HRS4

Daniel MacGregor is at it again...

New York Times bestselling author

NORA ROBERTS

introduces us to a new generation of MacGregors
as the lovable patriarch of the illustrious MacGregor
clan plays matchmaker again, this time to his three
gorgeous granddaughters in

THE MACGREGOR BRIDES

From Silhouette Books

Don't miss this brand-new continuation of Nora Roberts's
enormously popular *MacGregor* miniseries.

Available November 1997 at your favorite retail outlet.

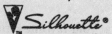

Look us up on-line at: http://www.romance.net

NRMB-S

The good ones aren't hard to find—they're right here in Silhouette Romance!

MAN: Rick McBride, Dedicated Police Officer
MOTTO: "I always get the bad guy, but no good
woman will ever get me!"

Find out how Rick gets tamed in Phyllis Halldorson's
THE LAWMAN'S LEGACY. (October 1997)

MAN: Tucker Haynes, Undercover Investigator
MOTTO: "I'll protect a lady in need until the
danger ends, but I'll protect my heart forever."

Meet the woman who shatters this
gruff guy's walls in Laura Anthony's
THE STRANGER'S SURPRISE. (November 1997)

MAN: Eric Bishop, The Ultimate Lone Wolf
MOTTO: "I'm back in town to find my
lost memories, *not* to make new ones."

Discover what secrets—and romance—are in store
when this loner comes home in Elizabeth August's
PATERNAL INSTINCTS. (December 1997)

*We've handpicked the strongest, bravest, sexiest
heroes yet! Don't miss these exciting books from*

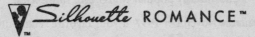
Silhouette ROMANCE™

Available at your favorite retail outlet.

Look us up on-line at: http://www.romance.net   MEN

You've been waiting for him all your life....
Now your Prince has finally arrived!

In fact, *three* handsome princes
are coming your way in

ROYAL WEDDINGS

A delightful new miniseries by **LISA KAYE LAUREL**
about three bachelor princes who find happily-ever-
after with three small-town women!

Coming in September 1997—THE PRINCE'S BRIDE

Crown Prince Erik Anders would do anything for his
country—even plan a pretend marriage to his lovely
castle caretaker. But could he convince the king, and
the rest of the world, that his proposal was real—before
his cool heart melted for his small-town "bride"?

Coming in November 1997—THE PRINCE'S BABY

Irresistible Prince Whit Anders was shocked to
discover that the summer romance he'd had years
ago had resulted in a very royal baby! Now that
pretty Drew Davis's secret was out, could her kiss
turn the sexy prince into a full-time dad?

**Look for prince number three in the exciting
conclusion to ROYAL WEDDINGS,
coming in 1998—only from**

Silhouette ROMANCE™

Look us up on-line at: http://www.romance.net   ROYAL

SILHOUETTE WOMEN KNOW ROMANCE WHEN THEY SEE IT.

And they'll see it on **ROMANCE CLASSICS**, the new 24-hour TV channel devoted to romantic movies and original programs like the special **Romantically Speaking—Harlequin™ Goes Prime Time.**

Romantically Speaking—Harlequin™ Goes Prime Time introduces you to many of your favorite romance authors in a program developed exclusively for Harlequin® and Silhouette® readers.

Watch for **Romantically Speaking—Harlequin™ Goes Prime Time** beginning in the summer of 1997.

If you're not receiving ROMANCE CLASSICS, call your local cable operator or satellite provider and ask for it today!

ROMANCE CLASSICS

Escape to the network of your dreams.

See Ingrid Bergman and Gregory Peck in *Spellbound* on Romance Classics.

©1997 American Movie Classics Co. "Romance Classics" is a service mark of American Movie Classics Co.
Harlequin is a trademark of Harlequin Enterprises Ltd.
Silhouette is a registered trademark of Harlequin Books, S.A.

RMCLS-S-R2